Catch the Saint

By Leslie Charteris

DAREDEVIL

THE BANDIT

THE WHITE RIDER

X ESQUIRE

The Saint Series in order of Sequence

MEET THE TIGER!

ENTER THE SAINT

THE SAINT CLOSES THE CASE

THE AVENGING SAINT

FEATURING THE SAINT

ALIAS THE SAINT

THE SAINT MEETS HIS MATCH

THE SAINT V. SCOTLAND YARD

THE SAINT'S GETAWAY

THE SAINT AND MR. TEAL

THE BRIGHTER BUCCANEER

THE SAINT IN LONDON

THE SAINT INTERVENES

THE SAINT GOES ON

THE SAINT IN NEW YORK

THE SAINT OVERBOARD

ACE OF KNAVES

THE SAINT BIDS DIAMONDS

THE SAINT PLAYS WITH FIRE

FOLLOW THE SAINT

THE HAPPY HIGHWAYMAN

THE SAINT IN MIAMI

THE SAINT GOES WEST

THE SAINT STEPS IN

THE SAINT ON GUARD

THE SAINT SEES IT THROUGH

CALL FOR THE SAINT

SAINT ERRANT

THE SAINT IN EUROPE

THE SAINT ON THE SPANISH MAIN

THANKS TO THE SAINT

THE SAINT AROUND THE WORLD

SEÑOR SAINT

THE SAINT TO THE RESCUE

TRUST THE SAINT

THE SAINT IN THE SUN

VENDETTA FOR THE SAINT

THE SAINT ON T.V.

THE SAINT RETURNS

THE SAINT AND THE FICTION
   MAKERS

THE SAINT ABROAD

THE SAINT'S CHOICE

THE SAINT IN PURSUIT

THE SAINT AND THE PEOPLE
   IMPORTERS

CATCH THE SAINT

Catch the Saint

BY LESLIE CHARTERIS

Two original stories by Norman Worker
Adapted by Flemming Lee

PUBLISHED FOR THE CRIME CLUB BY
DOUBLEDAY & COMPANY, INC.
GARDEN CITY, NEW YORK
1975

All the characters in this book are fictitious, and any resemblance to actual persons, living or dead, is purely coincidental.

Library of Congress Cataloging in Publication Data

Lee, Flemming.
Catch the Saint.

(The Saint series)
CONTENTS: The masterpiece merchant.—The adoring socialite.
I. Charteris, Leslie, 1907– II. Worker, Norman.
III. Title.
PZ4.L4774Cat [PS3562.E35] 813'.5'4
ISBN 0-385-09936-3
Library of Congress Catalog Card Number 74–25098

Foreword

The time seems to have come when Simon Templar cannot plausibly go on being contemporary, or else too many literary detectives smarter than Chief Inspector Teal are going to be deducing his present age from the internal evidence of several stories in the Saga that were highly topical at the time they first appeared, and in which the Saint was irrevocably linked with certain historic dates and events. And awkward questions are bound to be asked about how, in 1975 or later still, he retains the same exuberance and agility that he displayed forty and more years ago.

The only alternative to taking him into the realms of science fiction for a miraculous rejuvenation, if the demand for more stories about him continues, is to delve into his past for hitherto untold adventures of his earlier years—which, indeed, some loyal followers maintain were his best.

This, then, is the first experiment of that kind. Although the stories in this book are brand new, they are not set in 1975, the year of first publication, but must be regarded as having taken place before the world war of 1939. Any "dated" details in them that may be spotted by today-conscious readers are therefore strictly intentional.

LC

Contents

FOREWORD v

I: THE MASTERPIECE MERCHANT 1

II: THE ADORING SOCIALITE 80

Catch the Saint

The Masterpiece Merchant

CHAPTER 1

Every weekday morning at precisely ten o'clock, Mrs Evelyn Teasbury backed her shiny black Rolls Royce from its green-doored garage in Upper Berkeley Mews and embarked on her rounds of London and environs.

Simon Templar, that aficionado of the unexpected, that master of the unpredictable, never followed any such set routine. But he also lived in Upper Berkeley Mews, and in the course of the years since Mrs Teasbury's husband had died, he had often observed the old lady's departures. Hatted and gloved, impeccable in spite of reduced circumstances, she would back her well-preserved but ancient Rolls (obviously a major feature of her late husband's estate) into the street, leave it running while she closed the gleaming green garage door, and drive smoothly and slowly away. Her clothing and the car never changed, year after year, as Mrs Teasbury stiffly but gracefully mounted the stairs of her seventies. The garage door got a fresh coat of paint every spring, and Mrs Teasbury's hair became whiter and whiter; otherwise her contribution to the appearance and activities of the neighbourhood was inconspicuous but immutable.

It was therefore a big surprise to Simon Templar when he set out one morning in his own new, growling, incredibly expensive Hirondel and overtook Mrs Teasbury as she left her modest flat on foot. He had never seen her walk any farther than the garage before. He came to a stop alongside the slowly moving figure and hailed her with a cheerful "Good morning!"

They had often exchanged just about that many words apiece, and Mrs Teasbury, like all females, had been taken with Simon's dashing good looks and open pleasantness.

"Good morning," she said quietly, with a nod, and started to move on towards the corner.

"Would you like a ride?" Simon asked. "In fact, I insist."

He had recognised the dignified struggle between acceptance and rejection which had flashed across her wrinkled face. He was out of the car opening the door for her before she could reply.

"I'm very grateful to you," she breathed as he pulled away from the kerb. "Walking is a bit of a struggle for me these days."

"Is your car under the weather?" he asked.

He could immediately sense the tension that gripped his passenger.

"It's gone," she said. "I had to sell it."

There was something in the wording and the way she spoke that made him realise that she was admitting a personal catastrophe and not just a timely business transaction. She desperately wanted to tell him, or someone, more about it; she wanted to be questioned.

"You had to?" he asked. "I hope nothing is wrong."

It was normal, in the course of inflation and political fluctuation, that a person in reduced circumstances living on a non-growing income might find her circumstances getting more and more reduced. But Mrs Teasbury immediately confessed something more drastic:

"Yes," she said. "Wrong is definitely the word. I have been wronged. I have been taken advantage of and lied to and cheated. So I've been forced to sell my car in order to pay my bills." She hesitated, and Simon waited, driving slowly with no particular destination in mind. Mrs Teasbury had probably just come as close to crying as she would ever come in front of a relative stranger. "I'm not sure why I'm telling you this, except that I've

2

heard some wild tales about what you've done to criminals, and I feel that what has been done to me is a crime."

"What happened exactly?" Simon asked.

"I'm not asking for help. What's done is done. If you would please drop me off at an underground station that would take me to High Holborn I'd be most grateful. I have to go begging to my banker."

Simon continued driving nowhere.

"I realise you're not asking for anything," he said. "But I'd like to know what happened."

"I was given very bad advice, to say the least," she said. "A certain so-called art expert whose name I now detest advised me several years ago to sell some paintings my husband and I had bought. This was after my husband had died, and I needed to make some good investments. This art dealer told me that what I had would never be worth much. He arranged for me to sell my paintings through him for next to nothing, and to put money into several paintings that he assured me would go up in value. 'Skyrocket' was the word he used. This all happened over a period of years. I bought the most recent painting from him just last year."

"I can imagine the rest," Simon said. "The art treasures you bought turned out to . . ."

"To be rubbish," the old lady interrupted. "And I read in the paper a few days ago that one of the paintings I had *sold* to this individual for eight hundred pounds had gone at auction for nineteen thousand pounds. And this is only nine years after I sold it."

"Of course if you accuse your dealer of cheating you he'll apologise profusely and say he can't be right all the time.

"Exactly," Mrs Teasbury snapped. "That is exactly what he did say. But he deliberately took advantage. He talked me into believing that art works were the best investment I could make, and that his advice was the best I could follow. Over the years, he has underpaid me for the paintings I owned and vastly overcharged me for the paintings he sold me. Now I have nothing. It's my own fault. I should have gone about it all quite differently."

"Would you mind telling me your art dealer's name?" Simon asked very quietly.

She told him, and it was a name that was only vaguely familiar to him. She immediately added, "But there's nothing to be done. My solicitor, who was gracious enough to advise me without collecting his fee, has told me I have no legal recourse."

Simon Templar thought, but did not say, as he headed towards Kingsway, that where legal recourse left off was usually where his own endeavours began. As most guardians of the law knew, however inconsequential their posts and their locations throughout the world, Simon Templar was not exactly their comrade on the paths of licitness. While Mrs Evelyn Teasbury knew him as a handsome young man always dashing to and from his house at odd hours of the day and night, to those who dealt with him directly he was a renegade whose methods simply ignored the existence of conventional statutes which did more to protect the criminal than the criminal's prey. Yet his results were of a kind that could as a rule be heartily (though perhaps secretly) applauded by the police, the clergy, and other traditional sentinels of righteousness. Perhaps it was this invariable element of justice in Simon Templar's extra-legal deeds, and the fact that the beneficiaries of his forays were usually the weak and defenceless, that had earned him his nickname, "the Saint."

Julie Norcombe, like almost everyone who could read a newspaper in those days, had heard of the Saint, and had a general idea of what he stood for; but it had never occurred to her that he might take an interest in her problems, weak and defenceless though she certainly felt. It seemed she had spent most of her twenty-two years of life worrying about one thing or another. Was she too thin? Was she pretty or ugly? What would her mother say if she did this, or didn't do that?

On one particular night, however, she had something nice and solid and specific to worry about, and not just something that could be put down to what even she recognised as an irrational lack of self-confidence. Only two days before, she had taken the first great breathless leap from the maternal nest in Manchester and come down to London to stay with her brother, Adrian. The idea was that she could live in his Chelsea flat until she could test her wings and see what she wanted to do. Adrian, four years older than she, was no paragon of strength and stability, but he was conscientious and reliable, and she thought that he really cared about her.

So it was not like him to worry her by simply disappearing within forty-eight hours of her arrival. He had received a telephone call late in the afternoon requesting him to see a dealer about an order for one of his paintings. Adrian had not wanted to go, even though he was naturally pleased at the prospect of a sale, because he had been working all day in his studio at the back of the flat and was tired. He had had a quick tea and then left her, promising to be back within an hour or two.

But he had not come back in two hours, or three, or even six. Julie had grown at first uneasy, then frightened, not only for Adrian but for herself. In her mother's vivid diatribes, London would have fitted appropriately and unobtrusively somewhere between the eighth and ninth levels of Dante's underworld, so replete was it with thuggery, thievery, chicanery, arson, and rape . . . not to mention an atmosphere of general debauchery that would have corroded the soul of John Calvin himself.

Adrian Norcombe did not drink. In fact he had none of the vices traditionally associated with artists. He was neat and clean, trimmed his beard every morning, hung up his clothes, washed his dishes (until his sister took over that chore for him), and was punctilious about keeping appointments on time. It was totally unlike him to be late. No business haggling could have kept him so long. His sister was literally in tears at round three in the morning, and she practically ran to the door when she heard the shoes clapping and scraping on the steps outside. There was a chain lock, which allowed her to look out without exposing herself to one of the assaults so picturesquely predicted by her mother.

To her horror, it was not Adrian who stood outside the door, but three grim-looking men against the background of an equally grim-looking black car.

"Oh!" It was half gasp, half cry, as she slammed the door shut again and fumbled to throw the bolt.

Knuckles rapped insistently on the wood.

"Miss, open up please. Miss?"

"Go away or I'll call the police."

"We are the police. Special Branch officers. About your brother."

Julie now had to struggle to free the bolt again. But she stopped short of removing the protection of the chain. She peered out at the shadowy faces.

"What's happened to my brother? How do I know you're who you say you are?"

From outside, her own face, back-lighted by the yellowish glow from inside the flat, looked gaunt, her eyes abnormally large, as if she had been starved by something more extreme than post-war rationing. But when she stepped back a little into the room to study the card that one of the men had slipped to her over the door chain, and the light fell more evenly on her features, even the least discerning visitor would have observed that she was quite a beautiful young woman.

She peered out at the men once more for a moment, and then slipped the chain from its catch and opened the door. They came in quietly, removing their hats, already looking round the room with mechanical thoroughness.

"What's happened to him?" Julie asked, putting her hand against the back of an armchair for support in case the answer was too shattering. "Has he been in an accident?"

"Before we discuss this, I'd like to be certain who you are," the spokesman for the Special Branch officers said. "Presumably you're his sister."

"Yes."

"Do you have some identification?"

The other two men had begun moving systematically round the living-room, occasionally picking something up and putting it down again. Julie wondered if they should be doing that without asking her permission or producing a warrant or something, but she was too timid to protest. She got her purse and satisfied the officer that she was indeed Julie Norcombe.

"Please tell me," she begged. "What's happened? Do you know where he is? He's been gone for hours."

"I'm afraid I have some rather unpleasant news for you, Miss Norcombe. Your brother has been arrested."

The girl had to go further than to lean on the chair. She sat down in it like a puppet whose strings had suddenly been released. Nobody in her family had ever been arrested for anything. They had never even known anybody who had ever been arrested. The whole idea was as alien as a round of beer at a Temperance luncheon.

"He couldn't be," she protested. "Adrian would never do anything wrong."

"How do you know that?" the officer asked her, as his colleagues continued probing about the room.

"Because I know him," she answered. "He's my brother, isn't he? He's just not the kind to break the law. What is he supposed to have done?"

"Have you noticed anything strange about your brother's movements lately? Any changes in his habits or schedule?"

She wished that the man would answer her questions before asking more of his own, but she replied hesitantly: "I wouldn't know, would I? I've only been here since Tuesday."

"This past Tuesday . . . two days ago?"

"Yes."

The officer nodded as if she had confirmed something he already knew.

"Did you notice anything different about him? Say, compared to what he was like the last time you visited him here?"

"I've never visited him here before. He's always come up to Manchester."

The spokesman jerked his head towards the other two men.

"You don't object if we have a look round, do you? It's necessary."

"Well, if it's necessary . . ."

Julie determined that she would at least follow these detectives —even if they wouldn't tell her anything, she might get an idea what they were after. They went down the hall past the bedroom and bath to the rear of the flat, where Adrian's studio adjoined the kitchen. She was very glad she had done such a thorough job of cleaning the kitchen after tea; nobody could seriously suspect a man with such a clean kitchen of committing a crime.

"Can I do anything to help?" she asked.

"Just continue giving us your co-operation," said the officer in charge. "Do you have other relatives living in this area?"

"No, Adrian is the only one. All the rest are in Yorkshire. Except for some on the Isle of Man; that's on my mother's side, but only cousins. And then there's . . ."

"But in other words, there are none in London."

Julie shook her head.

"What about his friends, or people he does business with? Do you know many of them?"

"No. As I told you, I only just got here. I haven't met a soul." She tried again to assert her own right to ask questions:

"Where is he? Can I see him?"

"No. I'm afraid not."

They were moving more or less as a group from the simple kitchen into the paint-and-turpentine atmosphere of Adrian's studio. Adrian was a frugal man, but he had been more lavish with light bulbs in his studio than in the rest of the house, and compared to the subdued illumination of the living-room and kitchen, the place had something of the brilliance of a floodlit stage.

Curtains had been drawn across the large windows; the skylight reflected the easels, tables, stools, and colour-smeared boxes and cloths that were arranged round the room. Adrian Norcombe obviously was a traditionalist, as numerous sketches and canvasses showed. His style varied, it seemed, from Renaissance to mild Impressionism, but among the examples of his work there were no cubist conglomerations, no abstract shapes or explosive splashes. In the centre of the floor was his current project, a very large canvass resting on heavy supports, its central feature a very large rosy-hued nude girl lounging in a cowpasture beside some Corinthian columns.

The painting was the first thing that had aroused the interest of the two silent searchers, who stopped in front of it and surveyed the lavish contours of its central figure with more respect than they had shown the kitchen utensils.

One of them drew down the corners of his mouth approvingly. "I wouldn't mind being on that picnic."

"You can go to an art museum on your day off," the leader said brusquely. "Let's get on with it."

Julie felt her face flush, and she avoided looking at the painting or the men. Their behaviour seemed rudely undisciplined, and a surge of indignation seemed to send some extra courage into her system. She found herself speaking out almost sharply:

"I'd like to know what you're looking for. You can see that he's not a rich man. I mean, he's hardly been leading a successful life of crime, and I'm sure you won't find any stolen goods here."

"There are other crimes than theft," the officer said quietly. "More serious in the long run, perhaps."

The group moved back to the hall and into the single bedroom of the flat.

"What, then?" Julie insisted.

9

The Special Branch officer stood in the doorway with her as the other men went through the wardrobe and drawers, which contained neatly segregated allotments of Julie's and Adrian's clothes. Adrian had been sleeping in the living-room, turning over the bedroom to his sister, but his clothes were still kept there. The officer's voice was like a knife inserted slowly and quietly into this homely setting.

"Your brother has been arrested under provisions of the Official Secrets Act," he said.

"You mean, like spying?"

"The Official Secrets Act deals with espionage."

"But that's ridiculous," Julie said. "Adrian's never had anything to do with the government or the services or anything! He's got weak lungs and a bad back. How could he possibly be in a position to steal any secrets?"

"There's more than one link in a chain," the officer said mysteriously. "But I'm not at liberty to discuss this—and neither are you, Miss Norcombe." He was looking at her very sternly. "I must emphasise this most strongly. You must not tell anyone what has happened. The situation is very touchy, with important things still hanging in the balance, and it is absolutely necessary that you keep quiet about it. At least until tomorrow, after you've spoken to Mr Fawkes."

Julie was feeling unsteady again.

"Mr Fawkes?"

"Mr Fawkes is in the Home Office. You have an appointment with him tomorrow—or I should say today, at one o'clock. I already have the address and so forth written down here." The man found a piece of paper in his jacket pocket and handed it to her. "Mr Fawkes is the gentleman who can explain all of this to you. I'm sorry that I have to be so close-mouthed about it. But after all, it's only a few hours until your appointment. Just have a good sleep, but see you're not late."

A good sleep! Julie thought despairingly. She felt she'd be lucky if she ever slept again. Unwelcome though these men and their news had been, she did not want them to leave. The thought of being alone now frightened her terribly. When they filed out into the damp August night, she had to struggle to keep her mouth from trembling. What if Adrian really had been involved in something? She could not believe it . . . but what if he had? Shouldn't they offer her something more helpful than their spokesman's final warning, before he turned to go down the steps:

"Not a word to anyone, remember."

She closed the door, attached the chain, and threw the bolt. She must try to sleep, somehow. Only one thing held her in the front room, and it seemed to call to her silently, like a living creature with some awful hypnotic power: the telephone. She had to restrain her hand as she passed it.

This would be the first crisis in her life in which she would not be able to call for Mother.

CHAPTER 2

She had slept about four hours, and knew she looked it. She rubbed her cheeks as if that might bring more life to her face. It was five minutes to one, and the taxi that had brought her was pulling away, leaving her outside the building in Whitehall, where she was supposed to learn more about her brother's fate.

She entered as if the very size of the place made her feel that she should make herself smaller, and approached a desk that promised INFORMATION. She cleared her throat and said:

"I have an appointment with Mr Fawkes, in room 405."

The commissionaire on duty was rather small and stout, and very businesslike.

"What time is your appointment?"

"At one o'clock."

"Most of 'em are out to lunch at this hour, but if he's expecting you . . ."

He dialled a number on the telephone beside him, and tapped his fingers while he waited for an answer.

"Hullo," he said. "Is Mr Fawkes in? A young lady to see him." He cupped his hand over the mouthpiece and leaned forward. "What name, please?"

"Julie Norcombe."

She half expected his face to cloud over at the very mention of what now must be a notorious last name, but he went ahead as briskly as ever: "Miss Norcombe. It is 'Miss,' isn't it?"

"Yes," she admitted a little unhappily.

"Jolly good." He stood up after depositing the telephone in its cradle. "Take the lift to the fourth floor. Mr Fawkes's office is immediately to your right as you get out."

A few minutes later she was standing outside a door labelled "J. FAWKES" and "405." She knocked. The door opened, and a red-haired girl looked out at her.

"Miss Norcombe?"

"Yes. I have an appointment with—"

"Mr Fawkes is expecting you. Come in, please."

It was a large, impressive office, with solid heavy furnishings. Mr Fawkes's red-headed secretary was also impressive, though for her shape and proportions rather than any heaviness. Mr Fawkes himself was most impressive of all. He rose from behind his desk to a height of about six feet, and spoke to her with an accent that she associated almost exclusively with the BBC Third Programme.

"Miss Norcombe, do have a seat. It's good of you to come."

She was overawed not only by the silky smooth uncoiling of his phrases, but also by the grey at his temples, his majestic straight nose, the poise with which he held himself and gestured her to a chair, a little as if he were flicking a speck of dust from the air with the backs of his fingertips.

"Thank you," was all Julie could say.

She found herself wanting to make a good impression, wanting to equal Mr Fawkes in poise. He was a facet of London that she had imagined admiringly in advance, and now found completely up to her ideal. For a moment she forgot why she was there . . . but only for a moment.

"I'm sorry about your brother, Miss Norcombe," Fawkes said, sinking easily back into his chair. "I'm particularly sorry that the news had to be broken to you as it was, in the wee small hours of the morning. But that's the way we have to operate sometimes."

Julie glanced towards the secretary, who was now at her own desk on the other side of the room, absorbed in writing something down. Was she making a record of the conversation?

"It's all right," Julie said. "I just couldn't believe it. Adrian is . . . He just isn't . . ."

Fawkes looked coolly sympathetic.

"Appearances can be deceiving, as the cliché has it. In any case, we don't want to rush to conclusions about your brother's character. A man can be motivated by a great many things."

"I'm not sure what you mean."

Fawkes shrugged.

"Well, blackmail for example. Or financial problems. An artist may, for example, believe that he has such a great mission in life that he can rationalise almost any means of keeping himself going."

Julie broke in: "I beg your pardon, but please tell me, exactly what did my brother do?"

"Your brother has been detained under Section 48C of the Defence Regulations. What that means is that he is allegedly involved in activities aiding potential enemies of His Majesty. Foreign powers, in other words."

"How could he do that?" Julie asked cautiously. It suddenly occurred to her for the first time that if the police or whoever they were could mistakenly accuse her brother of crimes, they might suspect her too. "I really don't understand," she added, to emphasise her innocence.

"By transmitting information," Fawkes said, touching his palms together lightly. "That's just one possibility. A man can

13

act as a courier without actually doing any spying in the sense of stealing or compiling information. He may have very little knowledge of what he's doing, or why, for that matter."

Julie studied the man's face for some chink in the carefully controlled professional façade. She found none.

"But you must know what he was supposed to be doing," she said.

"I know more than I'm permitted to tell you. That's the whole point of this conversation, actually. We didn't count on you, you see. Since your brother was under surveillance, we knew you were coming, but you'll recall that you were a little uncertain until the last minute about exactly when you would arrive in London, and it happened that our own plans for your brother's detention were delayed for about a week by circumstances. Otherwise the whole thing might have been over with before you got here."

Julie felt momentarily hopeful.

"You mean Adrian might just be held for a few days and then let go?"

"That's a possibility," Fawkes replied. "Remember, his guilt hasn't been proved in a court of law or anything like that. But what I was really getting at is the fact that a number of people are involved in this business, and we have only some of them under arrest. The investigation is continuing. No doubt more members of the ring will be rounded up over the next few days. Meanwhile we have to keep the whole situation completely quiet. We need a smoke-screen of silence. I'm talking to you not only to explain the situation. My primary purpose is to make absolutely certain that you don't mention anything about this to anyone."

"Well, yes, but with people being arrested, won't the other . . ." She paused to grope for a word. "Won't the other spies realise what's happening anyway?"

"To some extent, of course. But if I explained the whole situation to you in detail I'd be violating my own orders. Just believe me: You mustn't say anything."

14

"What should I do, if somebody asks me about him?"

"In the first place, don't mention to anyone that your brother is gone. In the second place, if someone questions you as to his whereabouts, be vague about it and pretend there's nothing abnormal about the fact that you don't know where he can be reached at the moment. Artists are eccentric fellows, after all. Perhaps he's gone off to Cornwall to practice yoga."

Julie did not smile, though Fawkes did, slightly.

"How long do I have to keep this up?" she asked him.

He looked completely serious again, and thought before speaking.

"Possibly for several weeks. We'll let you know."

"Several weeks?" It was the first time Julie had raised her voice. "That's a long time."

"All you have to do is say nothing," Fawkes insisted. "You may feel it's best to go back home. I think I'd agree with you on that. It might spare you problems here."

"What would I tell my mother?"

"You can easily explain to her that your brother has gone on a trip."

"But where *is* he really? Adrian? What's happened to him?"

"I can't divulge that information. But you can be sure he's being treated well. When the undercover aspect of this affair is completed, he'll be given every facility for his defence."

"Couldn't I see him, or at least speak to him on the telephone?" Julie pleaded.

"I'm afraid that's quite impossible."

As if he had suddenly been made aware of the time, by a silent signal, Fawkes stood up. Julie got to her feet also, but hesitated.

"Will you at least tell him for me that I'm worried about him, but I believe in him, and I'll be thinking about him?"

He smiled.

"I think I can manage that." He came round the desk and walked with her to the door. There he paused and touched her

15

arm. His smoothly modulated voice was stern. "Miss Norcombe, I hope you realise that what I've said to you isn't just a polite request for your co-operation. I have to warn you that if you say anything at all about this to anyone beyond this door, it will constitute a breach of the Official Secrets Act and make you liable to immediate arrest. Do you understand that? And don't telephone me or come here again."

Something about the words *"beyond this door"* and *"liable to immediate arrest"* seemed so dramatically weighty that she felt smothered by them.

"Yes," she murmured. "I do understand."

"Good day, then. And thank you very much for your co-operation. Don't get in touch with us, remember."

As the door to room 405 closed behind her, Julie felt sure that her legs would never carry her to the lift. She felt lost, bewildered, and on the verge of panic. The adventure of London, which was to have meant a whole new life, had turned into a nightmare.

But by the time she actually turned the key in the door of her brother's flat again she was experiencing a new feeling, one that she had not known before in her life. Defiance would have been too strong a word for it. Determination had a role in it; so did curiosity, and courage. More than anything else it was simply a desire not to run away. She suddenly found, without actually having made a decision, that she was not packing her bags, but had bolted the door behind her and begun making a systematic search of every drawer, shelf, and cupboard in the place.

Long before that, "Mr Fawkes" and his secretary had departed Mr Fawkes's office in what would have impressed an observer, had there been an observer, as unseemly haste for so dignified a bureaucrat. "Mr Fawkes's" words, as he and his red-haired companion descended in the lift, would have seemed even stranger:

"Well, precious, I did that rather well, I think."

Precious nodded. "You should have been an actor."

"I am an actor. I'm sure she was completely convinced."

"I'm sure she was," the redhead responded. "The only thing that worried me was that she'd ask questions until somebody came back from lunch and found us there."

"It was beginning to worry me, rather. But I imagine that Whitehall luncheons tend to run behind schedule. I still don't observe any mad stampede for the filing cabinets and the dictaphones."

He said his last words as the lift reached ground floor and opened its doors. The place was relatively deserted. With his curvacious accomplice at his side, the tall man walked briskly through the lobby. The commissionaire glanced at them without interest or recognition. Outside, in the warm air, the erstwhile official adjusted his bowler hat and breathed deeply with a smile of appreciation both of the beautiful summer day and of his own success.

"There's still one real question," the girl said to him. "Do you think she'll really keep quiet?"

"Oh, I think so. She's got several good reasons for keeping her mouth shut. And if she doesn't, she'll damn well wish she *was* in the gentle clutches of the Special Branch. I would not like to see what our friends would do to her if she spoiled things at this point."

CHAPTER 3

As he paused before the window of the Leonardo Galleries, Simon Templar might easily have been taken for an art lover of casual quest for some addition to his collection. Not only was he in the most suitable Mayfair setting, but he also had the inoffensively arrogant air of a connoisseur, and he wore the clothes of a person who has both the taste and the money to patronise a tailor whose clientele includes an impressive number of princes, tycoons, and film stars. His trousers and sport jacket had the same costly simplicity as the white-painted fluted wood and gold-lettered glass of the façade before which he was standing.

But if anyone looked at him more closely—as several ladies did in passing—it is very possible that they would have sensed something incongruous in his appearance. He had none of the pallid softness of a typical rich city-dweller. There was certainly nothing of the aesthete in his movements or bearing. The deep tan of his complexion accented the intense, aerial blue of his eyes; there was not an ounce of excess weight on his body, which despite its entirely natural relaxation gave an impression of containing the pent-up strength of a drawn longbow. An observer might have guessed that this magnetically handsome Londoner, if he was a Londoner, had just returned from a safari in Africa, or had spent the English winter playing polo in South America.

The safari theory might have appealed the most, because this man had such an air of the hunter about him—a quiet but continuously alert watchfulness which gave the impression that even here in sedate Mayfair lions might wait round any corner.

One observer in the street near the Leonardo Galleries on this particular early afternoon did not have to guess at the identity or occupation of the lean, tall man who seemed momentarily absorbed in studying the art dealers' display. The observer, who was as plump and soft as the observed was sinewy, knew the other man's name, several of his aliases, and a great deal about his past activities. For the observer was Chief Inspector Claud Eustace Teal of Scotland Yard, and it was his business to know as many facts as possible about anyone relevantly connected with the world of crime and its borderlands of illegality. In Chief Inspector Claud Teal's territory, lions of a sort might really lurk at Mayfair crossings, and the most perfectly tailored gentleman might be a hunter far more deadly than any member—or leader —of a Nairobi-based shooting party.

Mr. Teal was feeling pleased with himself for having remained undetected by the man across the road. It was an unusual experience for him to be a step ahead of this particular individual; it was so unusual as to be a rarity akin to the invasion of Hyde Park by grazing giraffes. Mr. Teal, like a habitual loser in the stock market determined to grab his first small profit before it fades, decided to make his move—as his prey moved a step nearer the entrance door of the art gallery and looked as if he might go through it at any moment.

The detective wanted to say something clever when he surprised his victim. As his blue-suited form bobbed like a bubble through the traffic, he tried to think of something superior to "Boo!" or "Surprise!" or "Reach for the sky!" He did not want to say anything too threatening for fear of triggering his quarry's notoriously swift and accurate reflexes of self-preservation and finding his own rotund body suddenly sprawled on the pavement.

But Chief Inspector Teal need not have worried, either about the wit of his lines or his physical fate. No sooner had he gained the other side of the street and stealthily approached to within two yards of the other man's back, than without looking round his supposed prey sang out in an embarrassingly full voice:

"Hail, Claudius Eustacious, Conqueror of Soho, Emperor of the Embankment!"

"Templar," Teal said, "keep quiet!"

He said it in a choked voice, as if by constricting his own throat he might do the same to the other man's vocal cords.

"Such modesty, Claud," said the Saint, still without turning to look at him. "Don't you want all these people to appreciate your innumerable exploits in defending them against the barbarian hordes? I'm surprised that London didn't invite you to hold a triumphal procession long ago."

Teal, when flustered, was not good at repartee. Perhaps it was not his greatest gift at any time.

"Don't go into that gallery until I've talked to you," he said.

Now the Saint faced him, his blue eyes confident, laughing.

"You seem to have taken personal charge of everyone, Claud. I felt sorry for you standing over there in the shade, but now that you've come over to the sunny side of the street it hasn't done your disposition a bit of good. How about a drink? Would that help?"

"I'm not looking for any help from you for anything—" Teal stopped because the Saint was moving closer to the entrance of the Leonardo Galleries. "I've asked you not to go into that shop until I've talked to you," he repeated in a fierce tone, which worked wonders with his subordinates but in this case produced only amusement.

"Why are you so obsessed with my stepping into this picture palace, Claud? Don't alarm yourself. I'd have gone in five or ten minutes ago except that I knew you'd follow me, and I didn't want to embarrass you by luring you out of your natural cultureless element. I thought the sudden transition into the midst of all that art might prove too much for your undernourished soul." He peered intensely at the detective. "You do have one, don't you?"

"What?" Teal asked.

"A soul."

Teal groped in his pockets until he found a packet of chewing gum. Extracting a stick, he peeled the paper away, and as he spoke he used it as a pointer, for emphasis: "I have an idea what you're doing hanging around his place," he said, "and I know that this isn't the first time you've been here."

Simon looked guiltily through the window into the gallery's lush interior.

"You won't tell my mother, will you?"

"We've had a peaceful time lately, with you occupied elsewhere, and I don't want you stirring up trouble where there doesn't need to be any."

The detective was waving the bare powdery stick of gum in the Saint's face, and Simon drew back slightly and said: "Do you intend to do anything useful with that?"

Teal popped it into his mouth and jawed it defiantly.

"I'm not here to stir up trouble with you, either. I just don't want you to start it."

"How could I resist that graceful speech?" Simon said. "I'm

genuinely touched. Let's drink to a new era of peace and harmony. Luckily there's a pub just round the corner."

He took Mr Teal's arm and hustled him along the pavement. The inspector held back and protested.

"Fat men didn't ought to drink—"

"Think of it as a late lunch," said the Saint cheerfully. "On a hot day like this, who would take solid food so early in the afternoon?"

Chief Inspector Teal almost refused to go, merely on the principle that he should automatically resist anything that Simon Templar wanted him to do. For the man who had been looking into the Leonardo Galleries was that very Simon Templar who had upset Mr Teal's applecarts with such embarrassing frequency and efficiency in the name of a Robin-Hood standard of behaviour which the inspector felt was completely out of keeping with the integrity of British justice. Mr Teal also had strictly personal reasons for not appreciating the Saint's individualistic ethics, beneficial to humanity's more honest members though they might be in the long run. It was not fair that he, Chief Inspector Teal, should have to operate within the confines of the legal code and in consequence be made to look silly by a privateer who could invent his own rules as he went along. But on this occasion Teal had been on his feet for a long time, it was an exceptionally hot day, and if he had to endure the unpleasant experience of a confrontation with the Saint, it might as well be in comfort and with refreshment.

So a few minutes later they were sitting in the cool dimness of a saloon bar now largely deserted by the lunch-hour crowd of businessmen, salesclerks, and shoppers. Simon Templar raised his pint of bitter and toasted Teal: "To the continued success of our joint endeavours!"

He said it without detectable sarcasm, but Teal sipped his small lime-and-water suspiciously, somehow making it clear that he was merely drinking and not solemnising the Saint's sentiment with a ceremonial libation.

"Templar," he said, "word has come to me that you've been taking a lot of interest in the Leonardo Galleries."

"I like that," Simon mused. *"Word has come to me . . ."* He rolled it round his tongue like a vintage port: *"Word has come to me . . ."*

"I'd like to know just why you're looking into that particular place, and what you expect to gain by it."

"I should think it'd be your business to know the answer to the first part of that question without having to ask me," said the Saint. "The fact that you have to ask shows why your career has been, shall we say, a little halting. Fairly steady, but unspectacular. A little like a dung-ball being rolled up a hill by industrious but clumsy beetles. I'm sure you won't take offence at this constructive criticism, Claud, but your failure to know anything about the Leonardo Galleries also shows why you still, even at your advanced age, have to depend on me, a mere amateur, for so much of your information."

Mr Teal had turned the colour of a ripe radish, and might have damaged his teeth if his chewing gum had not been between them to cushion their impact.

"I probably know a great deal more about the Leonardo Galleries than you do," he rumbled, keeping the volume of his voice very low in spite of his anger. "The owner specialises in selling questionable works of art to rich clients who don't know any better. Of course he sells some good stuff too, but he makes his big profits touting so-called undiscovered geniuses—"

"Who never quite get discovered," Simon supplied. "He also likes convincing nouveau-riche English clients that some American artist is going great guns on the other side of the Atlantic, and that they just barely have time to invest in him before he catches on over here. His mark-up runs in the neighbourhood of 8,000 per cent in some cases. And he has other little tricks, like putting 'attributed to' or 'attributed to the school of' on some old canvas, or even on some imitation-old canvas, and running up the price."

"But you can't arrest a man for that," Teal stated.

The Saint smiled.

"Exactly," he said, and the smile continued to be transmitted to Teal through the unearthly blue eyes as Simon raised his beer mug to his lips again.

"Now see here, Templar," Teal said trenchantly. "That's what I'm getting at: If I can't arrest a man for what Cyril Pargit is doing, you've no right to do anything else to him either. He's not committing any crime."

"*Caveat emptor?*" murmured the Saint. "Well, I know of a case where Pargit got his hooks into a gullible old lady of seventy-three soon after her husband died. When Pargit met this widow, she had some fine paintings and a reasonable amount of cash. She needed to invest. Cyril Pargit told her her paintings were practically junk, generously bought them at junk prices, and sold her some real junk for most of her cash. So now she has had to sell her car to pay the rent, and God knows what she'll have to live on in another couple of years."

"So you *are* after Pargit!" Teal challenged triumphantly.

"I didn't say that," Simon replied calmly. "I'm aiding the ordained authorities by supplying information."

"Well, I hope you aren't going to put me in the position of defending a rascal like Pargit against you—which is exactly what will happen if you try to give him what you think he deserves."

The Saint drained the last of his bitter and stood up.

"Just to show you how honorable my intentions are, would you like to accompany me on a tour of brother Pargit's emporium? I apologise for my earlier slurs on your cultural status. You're obviously more knowledgeable about the local art scene than I thought you were."

Teal gulped the last dregs of his watered lime-juice and followed Simon out of the pub and down the street. The Saint suddenly drew up short, about twenty paces from the entrance to the Leonardo Galleries.

"Now there," he said to Teal in a low, admiring voice, "is a genuine Gainsborough."

Teal blinked.

"Where?"

"Right there. Take a good look. You'll probably see only one in a lifetime."

"That young lady?" Teal asked.

"That young lady," the Saint affirmed reverently.

She was standing outside the window of the gallery, looking in. She was slender but gracefully curved, her blond hair so fine that in the sunshine it seemed a flowing condensation of light rather than a material substance. Her pale skin seemed almost translucent, and although she had none of the obvious prettiness of a magazine cover girl, her features had an almost flowerlike innocence that made the elegantly outfitted women passing her seem as homely as cabbages.

"Very nice," Teal said. "Do you know her?"

"Only in visions, unfortunately."

"I always knew you must be truly balmy!" Teal said. "Do you really have visions?"

"Oh, Claud," the Saint sighed. "Let's go on and have a look at Cyril's sucker trap."

He herded the detective ahead of him through the gallery door. The display rooms were rich in thick carpeting and velvet drapery. The acoustics of the place were such that sound vanished almost before it could be perceived; moving there was like walking through puddles of silence. At the opposite end of the first large room a distinguished-looking man was speaking to a thirtyish woman who appeared completely mesmerised by his words. She herself looked as if a whole stable of grooms had been occupied for half the morning putting every platinum hair and dark eyelash and crimson fingernail in perfect order before she had allowed herself to be seen in the streets. Wealth seemed to have expanded her girth more than her mind, if her stature and blank facial expression were any indices. He walked her back towards the entrance door, his gestures spiralling softly like the smoke of incense. Her wide eyes and half-open mouth made her look for all the world like a fish that has already been hooked and landed, and is simply waiting to expire completely while the cook prepares the sauce.

"That's Pargit," Teal whispered in Simon's ear.

The Saint nodded to acknowledge this unnecessary information, and moved so that he could unobtrusively observe the dealer as he urged his enthralled client to admire a peculiarly bulbous lump of bronze near the window. Mr Teal was inspecting a large surrealist canvas in which snakes and elongated females writhed through a large Swiss cheese, and he was only vaguely aware that the gallery's entrance door had opened for a moment and closed, then opened again.

"Templar," he muttered, peering at the strangely inhabited Gruyère, "what do you make of this?"

When he got no reply, he looked round, and Simon Templar was no longer there.

CHAPTER 4

By the time Chief Inspector Teal noticed that the Saint was no longer beside him, Simon Templar was fifty yards down the street outside. Mr Teal's first thought was that he had moved into one of the other exhibition rooms. Pargit was still talking to his client not far away. Teal had heard nothing that suggested a hasty departure. He wandered, somewhat disagreeably mystified, farther back along the pathways of paintings.

Simon had left Pargit's establishment so hastily because of something only he had seen. When the door from the street had opened, letting in a sudden glare of sunlight not admitted by the tinted glass, Teal's back had been turned, and Pargit and his client had been in such an intent huddle that they did not even look round. Only the Saint had seen the Gainsborough girl open the door and start to step a little hesitantly into the gallery. Only he was placed so that the brilliance of the back-lighting from the afternoon sun did not dissolve the girl's features, and only he witnessed the swift and total transformation that came over her as soon as she had crossed Cyril Pargit's threshold. As she started in from the street she had been tentative but poised. Then, as her eyes fell on Pargit and his client, her body froze, she gasped, and Simon saw her pale face flush to a deeper shade. He might not have been observing her so interestedly if she had not been the same girl he had pointed out to Teal outside the shop a few minutes before. As it was, he had very little time to observe her now. Something had shocked her so acutely, or frightened her so badly, that she backed out the doorway before ever letting go of the knob, and hurried away without looking back.

The Saint had no idea what had caused her agitation, but he was drawn to mysteries as naturally as a shark is drawn to a stir on the surface of the sea. If he had been an ordinary person he could have explained her reaction in several theoretical ways that would have made it unnecessary for him to concern himself any further. If he had been an ordinary person who felt that her reaction was extraordinary enough to warrant some attention, he would still have run up against that great protective barrier reef of the human psyche that bears the marker "It's none of my business."

But Simon Templar was not an ordinary person. He felt that her behaviour virtually screamed for investigation, and that it was very much his own peculiar, individualistic kind of business.

So before anyone in the gallery area was aware of what he was doing, he had moved across the thick carpet with a casualness that belied his speed, and was once more out in the bright sunshine and heat of the street. There were quite a few people moving in and out of the shops all along the way, and many more just standing looking in the windows. It was the height of the tourist season; American accents at moments outnumbered British. In spite of the crowds, Simon caught a glimpse of that unmistakable blond hair a hundred feet or more away from him. The girl must have been walking very fast, almost running at times. She disappeared round a corner ,before Simon had come anywhere near her, but when he rounded it she was not ten paces away, just standing with her back to a brick wall beneath a red-and-white-striped awning. Her cupped right hand was pressed to her mouth, and her eyes, if they were seeing anything, must have been focussed on something far beneath the surface of the earth which only she could see.

The Saint slowed his pace as he approached her.

"I can help you," he said in the kind of voice he might have used to calm a nervous filly.

It took her a few seconds to accept the notion that he was speaking to her, and to realise that his words held something more meaningful for her than the general hubbub of the street. Her head turned so that her large green eyes could meet his, and for a moment he thought she was going to run again. But he could tell that she was more confused and overwrought than really frightened of him, especially out here in the open, where a single cry could have brought a dozen people to her aid.

She did not say anything. She just turned and walked quickly away. But the Saint, with two strides of his long legs, caught up with her and went along at her side.

"I can tell you're very upset," he said soothingly, "and I know it must have something to do with the Leonardo Galleries. There are certain things in the Leonardo Galleries that upset me too, and I don't mean the bad paintings." He took her arm gently but insistently and steered her away from the middle of the pavement. "Now that we know we have something in common, shall we sit down and decide where to go from here? There's a nice little cafe that looks your style."

She finally managed to reply with somewhat forced indignation: "I really don't just . . ."

"Your mother warned you about accepting sweets from strange men?" Simon put in. "I agree with her completely. But I'm not a strange man, and I'm not trying to pick you up. Talk with me for ten minutes, and if you want to drop the whole thing, I won't follow you. At the moment I'm all business."

Just before he slipped his fingers from her arm he felt her relax a little.

"Well, what is your business?" she asked. "I don't really understand."

"That's a very long story, but I promise you I'm not a white slaver or any nonsense like that. Let's have a cup of coffee or something before we go any further into it."

She allowed him, uncertainly, to seat her in the open at a round table under an umbrella. The Saint got a purely aesthetic enjoyment out of studying his Gainsborough girl at close quarters. He was touched by her yellow summer dress: There was something naive and childlike about it, just as there was about her, quite unlike the sophistication of the women he usually met in London. She was probably so shy because she was so undefended by artifice. Her eyes divided their time mainly between the pink tablecloth and the passing pedestrians, and only occasionally flickered across his face.

Only one thing gave the Saint some doubts about his approach: It might account for her reaction in the Leonardo Galleries if she was romantically involved with Cyril Pargit and had recognised the woman Pargit was talking to as a rival. Into such strict personal matters, Simon Templar would not have gratuitously intruded one centimetre. And yet, in that case she might prove a valuable source of information about the man who was doing her wrong.

"I'm sorry you've so obviously had a shock," he said. "Is there anything I can do to help just at the moment?"

"Do you think I've had a shock?"

"Haven't you?"

"Yes. I suppose I have." She met his eyes suddenly and looked away. "Are you a policeman or a detective?"

"No. My name is Simon Templar, and I don't think any occupational label would fit me."

For many people, the mention of his name would have been explanation enough, but this girl showed no immediate recognition.

"I have what you might call independent means, and my hobby is helping damsels in distress. You looked to me very much like a distressed damsel, and that's why I followed you. Now why would you ask if I'm a detective or policeman?"

A waitress brought two coffees, and strawberries and cream for the girl.

"It seems that everybody I've met since I got to London is a detective or something like that."

"Well, I'm definitely not," Simon assured her. "But I think I do have the distinction of having discovered a cafe that makes the worst coffee in the world. How are the strawberries?"

"Delicious, thank you."

"Would you like to tell me what was bothering you when you looked into that art gallery, and possibly also enlighten me about all those detectives?"

The girl spooned up another ripe strawberry, and ate it before she replied.

"I still don't know anything at all about you," she said.

"I don't even know your name," the Saint parried.

"Julie Norcombe."

"Well, before I start telling you anything else about myself, would you answer one question for me: How well do you know Cyril Pargit?"

The girl shook her head.

"Who's Cyril Pargit?"

"What about Chief Inspector Teal of Scotland Yard?" Simon asked. "Do you know him?"

"I've never heard of him. Who are these people?"

"What about the woman with the platinum hair and silver dress who was in the gallery when you came in? Do you know her?"

"No. I never saw her before. You certainly do ask as many questions as a detective."

Simon sat back in his chair and tapped a knuckle against his lips before responding.

"Well, then," he said, "the man who was talking to the woman with the silver dress—who is he?"

Julie Norcombe let her spoon remain in the half-finished bowl of strawberries. "He seemed to work in the place, and to be selling that woman a painting."

"Does that surprise you?" Simon asked.

"Well, yes."

"Why should it? After all, he's the owner."

"He owns that art gallery?"

"Yes, he does."

She was openly astonished.

"I don't suppose he has a twin brother, does he?"

"Not that I know of.

"I think the picture's developed enough for us to hang it up to dry," said the Saint. He leaned towards her and spoke swiftly. "You know Cyril Pargit, but you know him under another name. An obvious reason would be the married man trying to keep the girlfriend from finding out he has a wife. Girlfriend comes to London, stumbles on him in a place he isn't supposed to be, et cetera. The only trouble with that is that Cyril doesn't have a wife. But he could be trying to keep two or more girlfriends from discovering one another's existence. Is it anything that simple?"

"No," she said almost indignantly. "I'm not an absolute idiot. But you're right about the part where I know that man by a different name. Except of course that it just isn't possible."

"Tell me why."

"I can't."

"Apparently you think there's some danger involved if you tell me?"

"I . . . Yes."

"Well, suppose we make a trade. I'm going to tell you something which you could use to spoil everything I'm trying to do at the moment. All you have to do is tip Pargit off and I'm licked before I start. But I can't expect you to stick your neck out if I don't." He pushed his almost untasted coffee aside and rested his forearms on the table. "I believe that dear Cyril is a con-man and a fraud. In fact I know he is, but perhaps not in a way that makes him liable to arrest just at the moment. I've taken an interest in it because he cheated an old lady who's a friendly neighbour of mine. Does that help?" Julie Norcombe nodded. "Well, then, how about telling me why you're interested."

"I don't know what to tell you," she said tensely. "I've been told that I'll be breaking the law if I say anything. Let me see how I can put it . . . Something happened. Some people who said they were with the Special Branch came to where I live and told me not to say anything to anybody, but to see a man at Whitehall who would explain it all to me. I went to Whitehall and saw the man, and *he* told me not to say anything to anybody. He even told me not to tell anybody I'd seen him, so you see, I'm already getting into trouble. Except—the man I saw at Whitehall is the same man I just saw at that gallery . . ."

"Cyril Pargit," the Saint said.

"That's right."

"Very strange indeed. What department was this Whitehall man in?"

"Something to do with the Official Secrets Acts. I shouldn't be telling you this, but his name was Fawkes."

"And you saw him in Whitehall?"

"Yes. In an office there."

"And you won't tell me what it was that happened that got you sent to see this Guy Fawkes in the first place?"

She was very subdued, very nervous about what she had told him already and the fact that she desperately wanted to tell him more.

"My brother was arrested. He didn't come home the night before last, and they came and told me he'd been arrested."

"In connection with the Official Secrets Act?" Simon filled in. "What does your brother do that involves him with official secrets?"

Julie spread her hands helplessly.

"Nothing! Nothing at all that I know of. He's an artist. I don't think he'd know an official secret if he found it on his dinner plate."

Noting she had finished her strawberries and drunk all her coffee, Simon asked her if she would like anything more. When she said no, he signalled the waitress for the bill.

"What are your plans for the rest of the afternoon?" he asked her.

"I don't have any, now," she said. "I really . . ." Suddenly, like a cloud crossing the sun, tears filmed her eyes. "I think I'll just go home."

"I'll see that you get there safely," Simon told her. "It sounds as if you're up against a conspiracy of some kind. We may just have to form a little conspiracy of our own."

CHAPTER 5

On the taxi ride to Chelsea, the Saint pieced together the chips and splinters of information that Julie Norcombe reluctantly, fearfully divulged. By the time they reached her brother's flat he knew all about her coming to London, her brother's profession and personality, and everything that had passed since that evening when Adrian had gone out and not returned. Simon was playing with those scanty details in his head, trying not to rush his conclusions, but angling for different patterns, searching for possibilities that might be overlooked if he let his attention become fixed on one interpretation. Whatever storm was brewing, with Cyril Pargit near or at its centre, gave fascinating new dimensions to the problem he had set out to explore earlier that same day. Here was something even more intriguing than an encounter with a mere unctuous opportunist of the art trade who was technically guilty of little more than being too imaginative in his sales talks.

The Saint helped Julie out of the taxi and she was surprised when he paid the driver instead of getting back into the cab himself.

"I don't mean to push myself on you," he said, still very careful of this jumpy girl's apprehensions. "But I don't think we've quite finished our business yet."

His approach to her was hampered by the knowledge that she had a lot less reason to trust him than she had Mr Fawkes or the Special Branch officers who had called on the night of her brother's disappearance. Simon's biggest trump was the force of his own sincerity. With people who deserved no better, or in circumstances that demanded it, he was capable of the most outrageously convincing pretences, and of feats of simulation that would have aroused the envy of many a seasoned actor. But now, when he was being himself, and totally honest, his persuasiveness was really overwhelming. It helped to be as handsome as he was, to speak and dress as he did (people always seem to trust the educated rich), and to have such an air of self-confidence that you could not imagine him ever needing to do anything underhanded. But at the root of his power to draw people to him and inspire their trust was something intangible, an invisible aura which surrounded his body and flowed from his incredible eyes which was practically irresistible.

"I don't know what to do," Julie said forlornly, standing outside the still unopened door of her brother's flat. "Do you think that the Mr Fawkes I saw was really the man from the art gallery? I mean, I know he must have been, but it doesn't seem possible. He was there, with his secretary, in his office, with his name on the door, and the man on duty downstairs didn't think there was anything peculiar . . ." She suddenly paused. "Well, he did say that Mr Fawkes was probably out to lunch, but then he found out he wasn't."

"It'll be very easy to check this out," Simon said. "May I use your telephone?"

Any suspicion or resistance that remained in Julie's mind was being rapidly washed away. She hesitated for only a moment.

"All right."

Simon took the key from her hand and opened the door. As soon as he followed her inside he was intrigued by the mixture of North-of-England bourgeois and artistic individualism that characterised the place. It was as if two people lived there and had shared in the decoration—a very conventional middle-class old maid, and the artist who had tried to work in his own ideas wherever he could without unduly disconcerting his alter ego. The effect was comfortable but a little stifling.

"Has your brother always lived alone here?"

"Yes. He came down about five years ago and he's been here the whole time."

"There's one thing that I'm puzzled about." Simon smiled before he went on. "Well, one thing among several. I'm surprised you didn't recognise Pargit's name when I asked you about him."

"Why?"

"Well, what sent you to his art gallery?"

"Oh. I looked all through my brother's things, because I got the idea that I should find out as much as I could about him. I thought I might get a clue of some kind about what had been going on in his life before I came here, but I just couldn't believe Adrian had actually done anything wrong. So I started hunting round and I couldn't find much of anything . . . but on the back of one of Adrian's paintings, on the back of the frame, there was a sticker that said 'Leonardo Galleries,' and a price, so I thought he must have shown his work there or something, and I thought I'd talk to them about him. That's when you saw me."

They were still standing in the middle of the sitting-room. "Won't you sit down? Would you like some tea?"

"Neither, thank you," Simon replied. He paced round, his eyes taking in and his memory recording every detail of the room, just in case there might be something informative or useful there. "But if your brother had dealings with Pargit's gallery, surely there must have been more than a sticker on the back of a frame. Wasn't there any correspondence with Pargit?"

Julie shook her head.

"I couldn't find any letters or receipts or anything like that connected with art galleries."

"That's a little odd, isn't it? You're sure your brother really was a painter?"

"Is a painter, Mr. Temple—"

"Templar, but please call me Simon."

"I'm sorry. Yes, he definitely is a painter; I've watched him work since I got here. Would you like to see his studio?"

"Yes, but I'd like to make that call first." He still did not pick up the telephone. "You know, it's impossible that your brother didn't have any business correspondence, unless he never sold a painting. He did sell, didn't he?"

"Yes. And he used to mention where he'd sold paintings; you know, in his letters to Mother and me; but the names didn't mean anything to me and I don't remember them." She shrugged. "Probably I just haven't found all of his papers and things yet."

"Or else those Special Branch investigators purloined a few letters while you weren't looking, just to slow down *your* investigations."

"I didn't see them take anything."

"They wouldn't want you to, would they?"

She shook her head.

"I can't believe there are people running around actually doing things like that . . . to *me.* It's like something in a Hitchcock film."

"Let's try out this scene."

The Saint picked up the telephone and soon was being shuttled through the labyrinths of government switchboards.

"What was Fawkes's first name?" he asked Julie, his hand over the mouthpiece.

35

"Nobody told me. He was in room 405, though."

Simon spoke into the telephone: "I'd like to speak with Mr Fawkes, in room 405."

After one ring, a female voice answered, "Factory Act Administration."

"I was trying to reach Mr Fawkes's office," Simon told her.

"I am Mr Fawkes's secretary."

"In room 405?"

"Yes. May I help you?"

"I'd like to speak with Mr Fawkes. My name is Guido."

"One moment."

After a pause and a few clicking sounds, a male voice said, "Fawkes speaking."

"Mr Fawkes, I believe you're involved in administering the Official Secrets Act."

"No. The Factory Act."

"Then you're not the Mr Fawkes who had a discussion in your office with Miss Julie Norcombe yesterday."

"No."

"Do you know how I could reach a Mr Fawkes who's involved in the Official Secrets Act?"

"I've never heard of any such person, but of course . . ."

"Sorry to have troubled you. Best of luck with your factories."

Simon hung up and faced Julie, who was sitting on the edge of the sofa. "Mr Fawkes in room 405 is not even remotely connected with official secrets, and I doubt that your brother is either. It looks as if comrade Pargit suffers from repressed longings to be a member of the Civil Service, and spends his lunch hours playing bureaucrat. He borrowed Fawkes's office just long enough to talk to you and scare you into keeping quiet."

Julie was suddenly on her feet, her hands clenched. "Then where is Adrian, if he isn't really under arrest? Why couldn't it be the other way round?"

"You mean, could the Leonardo Galleries be a front for some Secret Service operation? I hardly think so. If they were, they wouldn't want a whiff of scandal about them. And if 'Pargit' were an undercover name for Fawkes, he wouldn't be swindling elderly widows as a side line. No—I'm sure now that your 'Special Branch' visitors were phonies. Why Pargit is going to these lengths is quite another puzzle."

"Then what's happened to my brother?"

Julie's voice was rising to a dangerous pitch, so Simon put an arm round her shoulder and made her sit down beside him on the sofa.

"Take it easy," he said quietly. "Your brother has probably been kidnapped by Pargit and his pals for some reason we don't know yet. The purpose of all the dramatic impersonations was to throw you off the track and—more than anything else—keep you from spreading word round that your brother had disappeared."

Now the girl's voice became more angry than hysterical.

"I'm a complete idiot! I believed the whole thing! And Adrian's probably *dead* or something!"

She started crying.

"Don't be so pessimistic," Simon said, trying to counter her despair with reassurance. "If anyone had killed your brother it wouldn't have served much purpose to use four men—men you might identify later—just to sell you on a fake version of where he'd be for the next few days or weeks. I certainly don't think he's dead. Assuming he's taken an involuntary leave of absence, whoever's got him must plan to keep him for some time—otherwise why go to so much trouble to stop you reporting him as missing? So I don't imagine he's in any immediate danger."

"But why would anybody want to kidnap him?" Julie argued. "Nobody in our family is rich."

"Maybe you can help answer that," said the Saint. "Any ideas?"

"No. I can't imagine Adrian doing anything except painting. He never had an ordinary job."

"Any strong political views?"

"No political views at all. He never joined anything."

"What about trips abroad?"

"He couldn't afford them. I suppose he's been doing better lately than he used to, but he certainly wouldn't have much spare cash for foreign holidays."

"It hardly sounds like the traditional picture of an artist's life. What about friends? Girlfriends?"

"He never mentioned any girls. He must have friends, but I don't know who they are. Adrian's very quiet."

Simon got to his feet.

"May I see his studio?"

Julie took him back through the hall to the room at the rear of the flat where her brother's sketches, paintings, and working paraphernalia filled most of the floor space.

"This is just the way he left it," she said.

For a long time Simon did not say anything. He moved about the studio, stopping for a while in front of each of Adrian Norcombe's creations, occasionally going back to one, comparing it with another. When he had made a complete circuit of the room, he went back to the large half-finished painting in the middle of the studio, and then turned to Julie.

"Is everything here his work?" he asked.

"I think so," she replied. "Do you like them?"

"Well, they're very interesting," the Saint remarked. "Every one of these paintings is very good." He leaned close to the big canvas, moving the tips of his fingers very lightly over the surface. "Technically, they're brilliant. He seems to be able to make a brush do anything he wants it to do. But he makes it do something different each time. I mean, each painting in here could have been done by a different man. There's no continuity in the style." He turned back to Julie, wanting to draw her out more. "Don't you agree?"

She nodded a little reluctantly, as if by agreeing she would be criticising her brother.

"Adrian said almost the same thing about himself," she admitted. "He said he couldn't seem to find his own personal style. I guess he learned to paint mostly by copying masterpieces in museums, and he never grew out of it. That's what he said. He's really made most of his money restoring paintings, or making copies for people. Even when he tried to paint something entirely his own, he said it came out looking like somebody else's."

Simon indicated the bucolic scene on which Adrian had been working.

"Titian in this case. Didn't he ever go in for twentieth-century styles?"

"I suppose not. He doesn't think much of modern painting. He loves the old masters."

The Saint nodded almost abruptly.

"I'd better be going now. Thanks very much for everything you've told me and shown me."

The suddenly almost formal way he spoke to her suggested that he wanted to break off the discussion and get on with something he considered more urgent. Julie took it to mean that he was dropping the whole subject.

"But what are we going to do?" she asked half frantically. "If my brother's been kidnapped we must call the police. That man Pargit—"

"Is our only lead at the moment," Simon interrupted. "He's much more likely to show us the way to your brother if he doesn't suspect anyone's on to him than if the police land on him. There must be quite a group involved in addition to Pargit if they had three men round here posing as Special Branch officers. And the stakes must be pretty high to merit all that manpower."

"But the police are trained to handle things like this, aren't they?"

"If it makes you feel any better, an inspector from Scotland Yard was in Pargit's emporium this afternoon, and I'm sure that even though he doesn't know about your brother yet he's taking a close and continuing interest in the Leonardo Galleries. Believe me, if Scotland Yard hears about the Fawkes caper it won't be a well-kept secret; somebody among the enemy is almost sure to get on to the fact that you're being questioned. Since it's so important to them to keep anybody from knowing that your brother has disappeared, it might be very unhealthy for him if he became a hot potato."

Julie stood in the living-room near the front door. She looked almost tearful again, tired and distraught and discouraged.

"Do you mean that we just have to wait?"

"No. I mean that in a case like this I'm a lot more confident in my own methods than I am in Scotland Yard's. Within a few hours after I leave here, Pargit isn't going to have a minute of privacy. He won't know it, but I'll know exactly what he's up to. I don't like waiting any more than you do, but if we're patient for just a little while we should be able to get a lead on what's going on."

"How will I know?" Julie asked.

"I'll be keeping in close touch with you—which would be a pleasure even if it weren't a necessity. And if you need to contact me, here's a number you can call. Keep trying until I answer. And one thing in particular: Considering our enemy's tactics, don't go anywhere with any stranger, even if he proves to you that he's a policeman or a detective—*especially* if he proves he's a policeman or a detective. All right?"

"All right."

Simon opened the door, stepped outside after a glance up and down the street, and smiled at her. "Don't worry. We'll find your brother. And as soon as I've contacted a couple of unsavoury acquaintances of mine and put them to work, I'd be glad to start giving you a personally conducted tour of London. You got off to a bad start, but you'll see what a great time a beautiful girl can have here."

"I don't know how a beautiful girl would feel, but I'd enjoy getting out."

Simon studied her face for a moment. "Is that false modesty, or do you really not know you're beautiful?"

"I know I'm not beautiful."

The Saint shook his head as he turned to go.

"I can see I'm also going to have to give you a conducted tour of yourself."

CHAPTER 6

"Hullo, Archibald," said the Saint cheerfully. "How would you and your creepy confederate like to earn a few dishonest quid?"

The little man was startled when the Saint slipped as soundlessly as an escaped shadow into the wooden chair beside him. Then his face split into a grin like a dropped melon, revealing the rotting pits of his teeth.

"Simon!" he said in a hushed voice trained never to be overheard by anyone more than three inches from his elbow. "Fancy seeing you 'ere! Now you're so bleedin' famous, I never thought you'd be down in our neighbourhood no more."

Simon looked around the dingy pub where he had found the little man at his accustomed table in the corner. Even in his thirstiest moment it would not have been to his taste. It smelled of stale beer and an indescribable smokey sourness which had required many years of aging to attain its present bouquet.

"I keep busy," the Saint said. "I don't have much time for visiting, but I'll always go out of my way to find a man who knows his work. I had a feeling your telephone bill might be a little overdue, with the usual result, so I came to find you personally."

"I'm honoured. Let me stand you a pint."

"Sorry; it's my round, Arch, but let me do it for you and Mr Wilson. Where *is* Mr Wilson? I recognise his cigar butt." Simon pointed to the glass ashtray in the middle of the scarred wooden table. "No man on earth can disfigure a cigar butt as nauseatingly as Mr Wilson."

Arch laughed in silent huffs. Even his merriment would never transmit sound waves to an eavesdropper.

"He's in the gents'," Arch whispered. "What's the caper? Do you really 'ave a job for us?"

Before answering, Simon went to the bar and returned with two pint tankards and a pink gin for himself, and then Mr Wilson himself emerged from the toilet and found his way over to the table. He had never, except possibly by his parents, been called anything but Mr Wilson. He was heavily built, with a fat stomach and the ponderous air of a retired alderman. His hair was greying a little, but his bottle-brush moustache was as black as shoe polish. He belched with surprise as he saw the Saint at his table, and there was a near verbatim repetition of the pleasantries that Simon and Arch had exchanged.

When Mr Wilson had been seated, and throats had been suitably lubricated from the pints of Bass, Simon stated his business.

"There's a man I want tailed. I don't want him lost for five minutes. I don't want him to part his hair without my knowing about it. I want to know who he sees and what he says to them. It's that simple. I know you two gentlemen have the talent it takes." He placed a ten-pound note in front of each man. "And now you have some encouragement. There's another twenty pounds apiece owing you at the end of the first twenty-four hours —or sooner, if you can produce some results before then. In fact, if you can get me what I want there'll be a generous bonus anyway."

Arch was already folding his ten-pound note into his trousers pocket.

"What is it you want, guv'nor?"

"Naturally whatever I tell you doesn't go beyond the three of us," the Saint said, with the faintest trace of threat in his cool voice.

"Naturally," said Mr Wilson, and Arch nodded.

"This man you're to follow is involved in a snatch. He or somebody working with him caused a certain person to become missing. He's my only real lead, although he's working with a group. I want him to take us to the missing person, or to take us to the people he's working with. Preferably both."

"Who do we tail?"

Simon did not speak Pargit's name. He had already written it, along with the art dealer's business and home addresses, on duplicate pieces of paper. He gave each of the men a copy, and then pushed a newspaper clipping between the two of them.

"That's his picture, when he was attending some artistic tea party. He's about six feet, speaks phoney Cambridge. I've got to warn you, by the way, that there may be a police tail on him too."

"Righto," Mr Wilson said, and belched again after draining the last of his Bass. "You can leave it to us."

"When do we start?" Arch asked.

"You just did," the Saint told them.

He was not by nature a patient man, although he had trained himself to wait when necessary. Since both Julie and his two hired bloodhounds had his home telephone number, he settled down there in Upper Berkeley Mews and spent what remained of the evening catching up on some reading. For a man with so little sedentary time, he was an omnivorous reader, and to that and a retentive memory he owed an encyclopedic knowledge of a fantastic range of subjects.

At about eleven o'clock he telephoned Julie.

"I hope I didn't wake you," he said, letting his voice and the fact that Julie didn't know anybody else in London identify him.

"No. I got in bed a little while ago, but I can't sleep. I'm so worried."

"I have two dependable men following our friend. If he's working with professional crooks I can't risk being spotted, and I hate wearing a false beard all day. Anyway, why should I do that kind of legwork when there are poor devils with beer-bellies to support who can't do anything else?"

Julie sounded more cheerful.

"Then you really think there's a chance of finding Adrian?"

"Of course. I'd enjoy seeing you while we're waiting, but it could be that the ungodly are having you watched, and if they recognised me with you they'd correctly deduce that you'd been spilling the proverbial *haricots*. Why don't you get out tomorrow and see some of the shops or go to a movie? It'll give you something to do to pass the time, and if you are being followed it'll help to convince your pals that you've swallowed their story and are just doing normal things for a girl who's just come to London."

"If I could pull myself together I should be out looking for a job," Julie said tiredly.

"What can you do?"

"Not much. I'm not a secretary or anything like that. I could look for a job in a shop."

"Julie, there is only one occupation for you. You were born to be a model."

"A what?" she asked unbelievingly.

"A model. You know, a photographer's model, or a fashion model."

"Stop teasing me. I don't have the looks for it."

The Saint sighed.

"Julie, it's always been a mystery to me how some women can be so unaware of what they really look like, but you take the prize. I can see that I'll have to get a second opinion before you'll take me seriously."

"Well, of course I'd *like* to believe you," Julie said, "but—"

"That's a start, anyway. I'll see if I can get in touch with somebody who can help you on the job front. Meanwhile, I'd better not stay on the phone too long, because my little helpers may get something on Pargit and want to call me. Give me a ring about one o'clock tomorrow afternoon."

"I will."

"Good night, then."

"Simon," she called quickly.

"Yes?"

Julie didn't say anything for a long moment.

"Thank you. Good night."

She hung up before he could reply.

The saint did not have to wait long for his investment in Arch and Mr Wilson to pay off. They had earned their full pay by eleven o'clock the next morning. At 11:15 Simon Templar's telephone rang, and the voice of Arch came breathily to his ear.

"We got something for you," he said. "You know about Sam Caffin?"

Simon knew about anybody who had been making a better-than-average living from crime for very long. As soon as a crook graduated into the upper income brackets it came to the Saint's attention as surely as the accession of a Texas oil driller to the millionaire class reached the records of mail-order purveyors of leather-bound classics and stock-market advice.

"Black market," Simon said, referring to Sam Caffin's original short cut to wealth, assuring Arch that they shared a common knowledge of Caffin's identity.

"Now he runs a mob in Soho," Arch continued. "What he's got to do with your friend, I don't know, but Pargit is set to meet Caffin tomorrow afternoon at two o'clock at Caffin's flat. One of Caffin's boys met Pargit on a corner of King's Road, and Mr Wilson got every word of it."

"It's definitely tomorrow at two?" Simon asked.

"Correct."

"Where does Caffin live?"

Arch gave the address.

"You've earned your bonus," said the Saint."

The next morning, just before noon, a telephone repairman stood at the door of the flat of Samuel S. Caffin and pressed the bell button. The spaciousness of the corridor, with its royal-blue carpeting and Georgian wallpaper, gave rich promise of what the humble mechanic was to find when he entered the flat itself.

The door soon opened to him, and a burly man with pimples and thick black hair asked him what he wanted.

The repairman, a Cockney, replied, "Telephone engineer." He consulted a slip of paper. "Mr Caffin?"

"No."

"Well, is Mr Caffin 'ere? 'E's supposed to know I'm coming."

The black-haired man jerked his head as a signal for the repairman to enter, looked up and down the outside corridor, and locked the door. They were standing in an alcove which opened into a large living-room. The hand of the eclectic but classically minded interior decorator was evident in every expensive vista. There was great emphasis on floor-to-ceiling drapery (with tassels), Tiffany lamps, and the white sculptured shapes of Grecian nudes.

"Sam," the black-haired man called, "he says he's from the telephone company."

Sam Caffin was sitting at a desk on the far side of the living-room, next to a high window. His sleeves were rolled up above his elbows, revealing arms thicker than the waists of some of his decorator's female statues. He was a very broad-shouldered, bull-necked man. His hair was blond, cut short, and his skin ruddy. When he turned to see what was going on behind him, a pair of gold-rimmed spectacles perched on his boxers' nose looked laughably incongruous. He was about forty, but his rounded features and smooth skin made him seem younger.

He seemed aware of the unsuitability of his eyeglasses, and jerked them off as he spoke.

"What's wrong with the telephone?"

"Didn't you get the notice?" the repairman asked. He was unusually tall for a Cockney. He too wore glasses, with thick corrective lenses that blurred his eyes to the viewer. A moustache shadowed his upper lip. "They're supposed to send you a notice in the post."

"I never saw it," Caffin said. He was brusque, but through im-

46

patience rather than belligerence. "I can't keep up with all the trash that comes in the post."

"I'm not supposed to be 'ere without you getting the notice first, sir; I'd best go get it and come back after lunch."

"I'm having a business meeting here after lunch," Caffin said. "Come on in and get it over with now, can't you?"

"I've got to change the junction box. We're putting in more modern equipment. With your permission I'll go ahead."

"You've got my permission," Caffin said irritably.

"Where's your telephones, sir?"

"Right here on this desk; and there's another one in my bedroom."

"I'll begin right 'ere, sir," the telephone engineer said.

He shuffled across the room, taking a route that required a kind of slalom among the statues and their fluted pedestals. As he approached Caffin's desk, where Caffin was attempting to turn his attention back to his paperwork, he stopped to admire a small beautiful Vermeer which hung on the wall. At least it would have appeared to be a Vermeer if Vermeer had ever signed his work with a small "AN" in the lower right-hand corner.

"Very 'andsome, sir," the repairman said.

Caffin glanced up from his desk and said, "Thanks."

"Very 'andsome indeed."

The telephone man shook his head admiringly, almost backed into one of the statues, and proceeded to look for the telephone box along the baseboard near Caffin's feet. Caffin tried to go on with his business. The repairman got down on his knees to inspect the junction, which happened to be only about two yards from Caffin's knees. Assuming that either or both men wanted privacy in their work, the proximity made it impossible. Behind the thick lenses of the spectacles, the blue eyes of the telephone engineer were hyperalert, and his fingers moved swiftly to open his equipment bag, belying the apparent clumsiness he had shown in getting himself across the room. His eyes, peering over the glasses which helped to obscure his normal appearance, measured the angle of vision that Caffin must have of the telephone junction. He shifted his position so that his body was between Caffin and the black container bolted to the wall near the floor. Now the junction container could be seen by the black-haired man who had answered the door, had he cared to look at anything so uninteresting; he had taken a chair near the entrance foyer and was perusing a copy of *Girl Parade* with scholarly intensity.

Quickly the telephone worker got the junction box open, disconnected the wires that connected it to the telephone on Caffin's desk, and then proceeded to detach the entire box from the wall and deftly free it from the other leads.

"See this 'ere, sir?" he said to Caffin. "This 'ole lot of equipment was defective." He displayed the vari-coloured innards of the box, disemboweling it to illustrate his point. "This 'ere, and this 'ere. Not worf a 'apenny. You'd 'ave 'ad all kinds of trouble soon."

Caffin watched impatiently as the repairman used a pair of needlenosed pliers to pull out little wires and crush small metal components.

"Are you supposed to be mending the bloody thing or smashing it?" he asked. "I can't do without my telephone."

"I was just showin' you," the Cockney said. "This thing ain't no use to no one now anyway. I've got a new one 'ere to slip right in an' tyke its place."

Caffin snorted as the telephone engineer tossed the wrecked junction box aside. It was now that the engineer hunched as close as possible over the wall connections. In his bag was a slightly larger box than the one he had just taken from the wall, very similar in shape and color. Its contents, however, were not standard issue of the G.P.O. and in fact could serve no useful purpose at all in improving the operation of Sam Caffin's telephone. The means by which they would cause him to communicate with the world outside his flat were most efficient, but had

48

nothing to do with telephones, and would have been disapproved of in the extreme by Sam Caffin himself. In fact, Caffin's immediate reaction, had he known what was in the new box, would have been to bring (or attempt to bring) to a swift, permanent, and unpleasant end, the career of the man who was about to install it.

Nevertheless the engineer went about the substitution as coolly as a garage mechanic changing a spark plug. As he worked, he heard the footsteps of the man who had been sitting by the door come quickly across the room, and a pair of shoes appeared beside him. He sat back on his heels to look up inquiringly, and his body, though seemingly relaxed, tensed for instant action.

"Thinkin' of learnin' the business, mate?"

"I'm just watching," the other growled.

His dour attitude seemed to be only the normal manifestation of his soul; it was not specifically threatening.

"Lemme show you wot the bloody fools 'ave done," the repairman said chattily. "You see this 'ere?"

Sam Caffin slammed a pen down on his desk.

"If you've got to do that now, could you do it quieter? What are you mucking around there for, Blackie?"

Blackie scratched his bepimpled face. "Just watching," he said.

"Well, go watch something else."

Blackie grunted and went back to his picture magazine. Caffin got up and left the room. In a minute the new box was attached to the wall. The wires to the telephone, however, were still hanging loose.

"Mr Caffin?" the engineer called. "Mr Caffin?"

Caffin reappeared.

"What is it now?"

"I can't finish this job right now. The idiots 'ave give me some wrong fittings. I'll 'ave to go back to the depot."

Caffin swore to himself, glancing at his watch.

"Can you finish before two o'clock?"

49

"Today?" the repairman mumbled, on his feet now.

"Of course today!" Caffin snapped. "You sure as hell can't leave me without a telephone until tomorrow."

The engineer looked dubious. Caffin reached into his trousers pocket, pulled out some pound notes, and shoved one out.

"That's to get it finished today."

"Thank you very much, guv; I'll do it. But I couldn't get to the depot and back before two o'clock even if I missed me lunch. I'll be 'ere as quick as I can."

"Wait until after three-thirty then, but get back here today."

"You can count on me, Mr Caffin, sir!"

At three thirty-five the telephone engineer returned to Caffin's flat. He was once more admitted by the black-haired guard. Caffin was not in sight, but the closeness of the air, dominated by a thick smell of tobacco smoke, was evidence that his business meeting had ended not long before.

"I'll 'ave this done in 'arf a mo'," the engineer said pleasantly.

Blackie showed no gratitude for the announcement, and went off to the other side of the room to stimulate his brain with a copy of *Frilly Frolics*. The repairman detached the container he had left on the wall. Inside, he could feel the small wire recorder still running soundlessly. He shut it off, put it in his bag, and five minutes later had restored Sam Caffin's telephone to perfect working order.

As he was seen to the door by the heavy-set watchman, he said: "Tell Mr Caffin ta for the quid, and tell him I'll be drinkin' to 'im with it tonight."

CHAPTER 7

"I can't believe it," Julie Norcombe breathed. "I just can't believe what Adrian has got mixed up in."

"It's quite a set-up, isn't it?" Simon admitted.

He had listened to the recording before bringing it over to Julie's flat, so he knew that there was nothing more to hear but a monotonous kiss. He leaned forward and killed the sound with a touch of one long finger.

"It must mean that Adrian's safe, then," Julie reasoned in momentary rapture.

"It sounds as if he's as safe as the crown jewels in the Tower of London," Simon agreed. "He's so much safer than the average citizen that he could probably get cut-rate life insurance . . . at least for the next few weeks."

The possibly ominous connotations of Simon's final phrase were lost on her. She was too concerned with the more glaring facts of Pargit's meeting with Caffin in Caffin's flat.

"But Adrian's a *prisoner!*" she persisted. "What if they don't feed him well? Or if they don't get him his stomach pills? He has a very nervous stomach. Or if they do terrible things to him . . . like beat him, or . . ."

Simon raised a soothing hand.

"My dear," he said, "if you were entertaining me as an involuntary artist in residence, and I was worth approximately half a million pounds to you, would you feed me crusts and beat me with andirons? No, you certainly would not. You would make me as comfortable as possible, cater to my hypochondria, lavish my pet medicines upon me, and feed me all my favourite dishes. In short, you'd try to keep me as happy and calm as possible, so that my hands would be steady and my brain operating at peak efficiency."

Julie whirled from a position she had taken near the front window, came across the room, and sat down facing Simon.

"But I don't even understand why they've got to have my brother kept a prisoner so he can touch up some old Rembrandt. All I can make out from that recording is that this art-gallery man who tricked me, and a lot of gangsters from Soho, have all got together about some painting and kidnapped my brother. I mean, if you look past all those niggling little details about who goes where when, and who pays who what, that's what it comes to, doesn't it?"

"Perhaps I'd better try to clarify a few points?" Simon said patiently. "I've listened to this tape several times now, and you've just had your first impression. And you were asking me so many questions while it was playing that you missed half of it anyway."

"I'm sorry," Julie pouted.

"All right. Now listen. I'll admit that it isn't always too clear from those discussions on the tape, but if you put together all the bits and pieces and use your noodle, this is the general picture: Our friend Pargit, proprietor of the Leonardo Galleries and your brother's sometime agent, had an amazing piece of luck. Not long ago, someone brought him a very old and very dirty painting and asked him to have it cleaned up and restored. We don't know anything about this client, but it was probably some artistically naive soul who inherited the thing from an aristocratic uncle, or found it in the attic of the family manse. Anyway, the person who trustingly lugged this painting into the Leonardo Galleries had no idea when it was painted or who painted it, but he hoped it might be worth something and he asked Pargit to identify and value it while he was having it restored."

"I didn't hear all *that,*" she said.

"Well, naturally Pargit and Caffin aren't going to recite the whole history of the deal in the course of their meeting, since they both know about it. But when you listen to this tape again you'll see that I'm right."

"Sorry," Julie said.

"Stop saying you're sorry all the time."

"All right. Sorry."

Simon breathed deeply and went on: "You can imagine Pargit's feelings when he discovered that he had been handed a genuine, original Rembrandt—a work that had dropped out of sight for a couple of hundred years and now was plumped into his unworthy lap like manna from heaven. So what does Pargit do? What he does *not* do is rush to the telephone to give the owner of the painting the glad tidings. Instead he tells the client that it's going to be several weeks before the restoration is completed and the canvas is identified . . . but meanwhile the client shouldn't get his hopes up, because it's pretty certain that the painting is by some insignificant imitator of one of the great masters.

"Now, as we know, comrade Pargit is a man who hasn't enjoyed outstanding success in overcoming the sin of covetousness, and he has no scruples about how he makes his profits. But what can he do? He can't just run off with the unknown Rembrandt, or pretend he's misplaced it. So he comes up with a brainstorm: He will have a duplicate painting done, a fine imitation of the real Rembrandt. This forgery will be suitably aged by the best dishonest methods. Then it will be presented to the client, and the client will be told that what he's getting is of course the restoration of his painting. The client will believe that he has his old canvas back looking much prettier than it did when he brought it in, and Pargit will keep the real Rembrandt. The client will be told that his painting turned out to be by a minor artist of the Rembrandt school, but not by Rembrandt himself. Cyril is now free to take the original genuine Rembrandt to the States and sell it for at least half a million. Do you get the point now?"

Julie nodded.

"And so they've got Adrian painting a copy of the Rembrandt?"

"Because Pargit knew his talent for imitation," Simon affirmed. "And that's probably one of the main reasons Pargit needed to bring Caffin in on the deal. Cyril isn't a strong-arm type himself. Those were Caffin's boys who visited you here the night Adrian didn't come home, and they're the ones who'll be making Adrian comfortable while he works."

"But why would Adrian do it?" she protested. "He mayn't be a great artist yet, but I know he wouldn't be a crook."

"Not even if they gave him a sales talk about what they might do to you if he didn't co-operate?"

Julie sat pondering for a moment, then abruptly raised her eyes to meet Simon's: "What'll they do with him when he's finished the painting?"

"I'm sorry you asked that question," the Saint replied. "I'm not sure that Pargit knows yet. He's probably hoping that things will work out so that he can just let Adrian go when it's all over. Your brother won't be told everything that's going on. Pargit may think that a pay-off and a warning to keep his mouth shut will be enough. But Caffin's a cautious type; and a rougher type. I'm afraid he may come up with a more drastic way of guaranteeing that Adrian will keep the secret."

Julie jumped to her feet.

"We can't just sit here talking about it! We'll have to get the police, and . . ." She started towards the telephone, changed her mind after two steps, and swarmed over the wire player with all ten fingers. "We even heard where they're keeping him. Let's play it back. How do you work this thing?"

"You're going to feel awfully silly if you erase the evidence," said the Saint with dry restraint.

But Julie had managed to light upon the rewind control, and the tape responded with shrill backward gibberish. She kept pushing at the side of it as if that could prod it to go faster.

"If you want to become a model you'll have to learn what to do with your hands," Simon remarked.

The conspicuous members of her anatomy upon which he was commenting flapped near his face like a pair of distraught pigeons.

"How'll we find the place where they talk about where he is?" Julie begged.

"Just wait a few more seconds."

As if he could somehow make sense out of the high-pitched squawking of the reversed wire, the Saint sat alertly watching the machine. Then reached out and with a quick movement brought the rewind to a halt.

"I'd better ring up the police now," Julie said. "We'll be hunting through that recording all night."

"No we won't," Simon contradicted. "Listen."

He started the tape forward, just at the moment in the clandestine meeting when Caffin ended a sentence with: *"so everything is going fine, but the sooner you can get your blooming Rembrandt Junior to finish his job the happier I'll be,"* and Pargit began a sentence with: *"Very well. How exactly do I find this place where you're keeping him?"*

Julie gaped at Simon, pointing at the recorder.

"Now how in the world did you know exactly where to stop it?"

"Being born almost superhuman is a big help," he said modestly.

"Oh, you!"

"We're missing the whole thing," he said, and ran the wire back so that they could hear Pargit ask his question again.

Caffin's voice replied: *"One of my boys can give you a ride when you want it."*

"I'm perfectly capable of driving myself down there," Pargit insisted. *"Norcombe's not your personal property. And that's my Rembrandt you've got down there."*

"Fifty per cent yours," Caffin corrected. *"But as far as I'm concerned, Rembrandt Junior is all yours. He's more trouble than a whole bloody old folks' home."*

"Eccentric type," Pargit agreed. *"How do I find him?"*

"Like you were going to Bournemouth on the road round the top of the New Forest. But when you come to the River Avon you continue on across it into Dorset. Then . . . you'd best look for The Happy Huntsman on your right after you . . ." Caffin must have moved across the room, for his voice faded and the next few words were indistinct. *". . . old road between stone walls. It's an old farmhouse, the only place round, stone like the walls, with a red kind of thing in front where there used to be a well."*

"I'll recognise it."

"Don't expect a candle burning in the window for you. There's only a couple of rooms we use, upstairs. Just to be sure none of my chaps bashes you, knock on the front door like this—three

times fast, three times slow." Knuckles rapped on wood. *"And don't try walking in until somebody opens up for you."*

Simon shut off the recorder. "That's it. Everything but a map."

"May I call the police *now?*"

"We are not going to call the police," said the Saint firmly. "And in case you get any ideas about calling them when I'm not listening, I can assure you that you'll be putting your brother's life in serious danger."

"Why?" she demanded.

"Because he's the most damaging evidence round, and a lot more trouble to hide than a painting. If that gang gets any idea that the kitten is out of the sack, you can credit yourself with making him instantly expendable."

Julie was stymied. She tried to think of some retort, then crossly folded her arms.

"And I suppose you can take care of the whole thing perfectly all by yourself?"

"I think so," the Saint replied calmly.

"Well, when?"

"In the morning. Your brother's safe for now, and there's something else I want to do tonight."

He left her still questioning and protesting, but more or less resigned to the necessity of obeying his orders.

"If you can't sleep, pack a few things," he told her. "Including some walking shoes." He paused at the door. "Do you enjoy watching birds?" he asked.

"Birds?" she exclaimed, in the final throes of exasperation.

"Just a thought," he said lightly. "See you in the morning. Eat a good breakfast."

When he arrived to pick her up, at 9:30 in the morning, she was waiting at the door with an inexpensive suitcase already in the hall.

"Beautiful day for a drive, isn't it?" he drawled. "You look lovely. The weather's perfect. What more could a man ask?"

In his festive mood he suddenly swept up her hand and kissed it. She blushed but did not pull away.

"You look very pleased with yourself, I must say," she remarked. "Did you enjoy yourself last night?"

"Immensely!"

He picked up her suitcase, watched her lock the door, and led the way briskly out to his waiting Hirondel.

"Out on the town, I suppose," she said jealously.

"As a matter of fact, no. I was breaking and entering."

"Breaking and entering *what?*" she asked with alarm.

"The Leonardo Galleries."

She sank into the passenger seat, looking a little stunned. Only after Simon had gunned the engine to life and pulled away from the kerb did she manage her next question.

"You don't mean that you actually broke in there?"

"That's exactly what I do mean." He slipped the car into second gear and it hurtled forward breath-takingly. "There were one or two things I wanted to confirm. The most interesting fact I uncovered was that the owner of the Rembrandt, who doesn't yet know it's a real Rembrandt, is Lord Oldenshaw. You've heard of Lord Oldenshaw? A very rich gentleman, and soon to be a lot richer when he gets his painting back."

"How did you get in that place?" Julie asked.

"Oh, I decoyed a constable, picked a lock, then just pulled out my flashlight and settled down to go through Cyril's files. Then I put everything back just the way it had been before I got there, locked the door behind me, and went home and had a nightcap."

Julie continued to stare at him.

"I've been in such a daze," she said. "I've let you take charge as if you had a right to, and yet you still haven't told me anything about yourself. Except now you talk about burgling an art gallery as if it were like making a phone call. And the way you got that recording—"

"I told you my real name," he said. "Apparently it didn't ring

57

a bell. I may have to get a new press agent. Would it help if I mentioned that a few people also call me the Saint?"

He hadn't actually expected her to give an imitation of a punctured balloon, but that was the approximate result.

CHAPTER 8

"There it is!" Julie cried, scooting forward on the car seat. "There, I can see the sign!"

"The Happy Huntsman," Simon acknowledged blandly, without easing the pressure of his foot on the accelerator.

Julie's head turned to keep her eyes on the old inn as the Hirondel sped past it. Over her pretty face came contours of dismay such as might distort the countenance of a lady watching her fallen handbag disappear in the wake of an ocean liner.

"Why didn't you stop?" she asked unbelievingly.

"Terrible place," Simon remarked, jerking his head back in the direction of the now-vanished building. "Even the huntsman wasn't really happy there, by the look on his face."

Julie stiffened her back and glowered at the road, a slender band of pavement which had zigzagged through a brief kink where it passed the fieldstone structure of The Happy Huntsman, but now flowed smoothly as an old river through rich pastures grazed by lazy cows.

"You've been making a joke out of this ever since we started out from London this morning," she said. "I'm sorry I can't fancy this a picnic, as you seem to. We must have spent at *least* an hour and a half over lunch when we could have got by just as well on a sandwich, and at one tenth the cost. How you can even keep this car on the road after all that wine, I can't imagine. And now you've roared right past the one place we know of that's near my brother."

"You underestimate my capacity to incorporate wine harmoniously into my system as much as you underestimate my good judgement," said the Saint placidly.

Julie glanced at the chiseled lines of his tanned face against the blurred background of sky and green fields. His strong fingers lay easily but with perfect control along the steering wheel of the powerful car. She could not keep her eyes on him without being tempted into renewed confidence. Her voice went on almost pleadingly after a moment, nervous strain giving way to an only slightly sarcastic supplication: "My brother. Adrian. Remember him? He's a prisoner around here somewhere."

"And we'll have a much better chance of finding him," Simon answered, "if we don't stay at an inn which Caffin considers a landmark. If we'd stopped there we might very well get found ourselves—by Pargit if he comes out to check on your brother's progress in his artistic endeavours. Also, Caffin and his mob may even have connections with the place. And furthermore, if you're still not satisfied, I'd rather not advertise our presence in the neighbourhood anyway."

"I'm satisfied," Julie sighed grudgingly. "Where are we going?"

"To the nearest hotel that offers decent accommodation to a bird watcher and his nature-loving sister. There happens to be one . . ."

"Sister?" she echoed.

"Yes, sister." He defined: "Sister: A female born to the same parents as another person. Also, a nun or head nurse. But I had in mind the first meaning of the word. Unless you're tired of being somebody's sister, in which case I'd be glad to take you along as my bride. You've been Adrian's sister for so long you might find a change of roles refreshing."

She found it hard to resist the light-hearted sparkle in his eyes, but she made herself respond coldly.

"I think I'd better start as your sister."

"And work your way up," agreed the Saint encouragingly. "Not a bad idea, if you can remember not to blow the gaff by calling me 'darling.' "

"That's one thing I shall *never* call you," she announced primly.

The highway snaked gently from the open pastures into a grove of tall old trees, where gilt lettering on the varnished wood of another sign announced the presence of the Golden Fleece Hotel.

Simon slowed down and came to a stop in front of the building, whose red-shuttered windows peered as quietly out through the trees as did the eyes of an old man who regarded them from a bench outside the public bar.

"Remember," Simon told Julie, "bird watchers. Brother and sister."

"What name do we use?" she asked.

He glanced again at the name of the hotel.

"Jason," he decided. "Simon and Julie Jason."

They strolled from the car across the lush green lawn to the old fellow in the chair, who acknowledged their arrival with an almost indetectible inclination of his bald head. His chin was less bald than his head, for it looked as if he had shaved himself with a chip of poorly sharpened flint that had left patches of stubble in some areas and in others had scraped away most of the skin. His eyes were red as he waited to see what the world and the road and the hours would bring.

"Good afternoon," Simon greeted him cheerfully. "We've come from London to watch birds."

The elder received this news with an impassivity evolved through many years of witnessing every form of human folly.

"There do be birds here," he pronounced.

"We'll be walking through the woods and fields studying them," Simon explained further, satisfied that this information would be spread throughout the countryside before nightfall. "Are you the owner of this establishment?"

Seeing that this Londoner was a man of poor but flattering judgement, the old man brightened up a little, admitted that he had no business connection with the hotel, and pointed the way to the main entrance.

Simon made quick work of getting a pair of rooms for himself and Julie, admitting no more than their aliases, their fictitious relationship, a bogus address, and their avian interests. If the plump soft-spoken woman who registered them had any doubts about their identity or purposes she kept them to herself as she ushered them up the creaking stairs to their adjoining accommodations.

"I hope you'll be comfortable," she said, and left them, while a husky teen-aged girl brought in two suitcases which she would not permit Simon to touch until she had deposited them at his feet.

Every floorboard and timber of the Saint's room seemed to have slowly gone its separate eccentric way during the centuries since the inn had been built, but the crazy tilts and angles of the place had a kind of informal friendliness that no shiny modern motel would ever achieve. Simon put his elbows on the warped windowsill, from where he could look out over his parked car and the surrounding landscape, and called to Julie, whose head soon appeared at the neighbouring window.

"We'd better get going," he said. "The late afternoon is a very good time for finding birds."

The particular bird's nest which they were seeking was much less elusive than many a naturalist's objective. First Simon had the directions that had brought them this far, and next he had the benefit of a local's knowledge of the terrain, for the old man he had first spoken to on their arrival was still on his bench when they came out of the hotel in their hiking clothes.

"I wonder if I could bother you for a little information?" Simon asked him. "I understand that a blue-billed twit was seen recently between here and The Happy Huntsman. An acquaintance of mine says he heard they were nesting near an old stone farmhouse. I don't believe anyone lives there. A road leads up to it between stone walls, and it has something like a red well in front."

The old man pursed his lips and rubbed the top of his cranial dome.

"Sounds like the old Benham farm," he mused. "But I never heard of no what-did-you-call-ems there."

"Blue-billed twits," Simon repeated gravely. "They were supposed to be extinct. That's why we're keen to get on their trail right away."

"You eat them?" asked the elder.

"No," Simon said airily. "We just watch them." The old man's subtle change of expression implied that Simon had just admitted to some indecency which, however, could not be openly condemned in a foreigner. "Could you tell us how to get to the Benham farm?" the Saint asked.

"Just down the road about a mile, on your left. You'll see the entrance opposite a sign for The Happy Huntsman. But you can't see the house from the highway."

Simon located the wall-bordered old side road that the man had described, went past it, turned round at an inconspicuous place, and drove past the road's entrance again, parking a quarter of a mile west of it so that he and Julie could reconnoitre with a flanking movement through the woods.

"If you like," he told her, "you can wait in the car."

She considered that suggestion unworthy of a reply, and strode off ahead of Simon into the woods until she stepped in a hole and fell to her knees. He lifted her, red-faced, to her feet, and led the way north from the highway along what seemed to be a public path. Before very long, they came to the top of a knoll shaded by tall trees, and far down to the right across an open field they could see a stone house.

"That must be it!" Julie said excitedly.

Simon could see the trace of the old road leading up to the house. Lifting the field-glasses which hung round his neck, he focussed on the house itself. Stone. Two storeys. Facing south towards the highway. And in front of it, a trace of something red which must have been the roof of a well.

Satisfied, he stood like a general planning a battle. The cleared fields to the north of the house gave no cover. But behind the building were thick woods, extending west to join the forested area where they were now standing.

"When it's dark," he said as much to himself as to her, "I'll come back this way, cross over through those trees to the north, and come up behind the house."

"And then what?" Julie challenged. "Take it by storm?"

"Take it in my own way," he said calmly, raising the binoculars to his eyes again.

"Just knock on the door and tell them to surrender?" she persisted. "What if there are a dozen of them down there? Do you see anybody?"

"No, but I'm sure they'd never let Adrian get lonely. They keep to themselves, I imagine, in those two upstairs rooms Caffin mentioned on the tape. Not nature-lovers, these boys."

"Then how will you get in, or get them out?"

"I think your idea was quite a good one: I'll just knock on the door."

"But—"

"Could you be quiet a minute, please? I see better when I'm not listening."

For a long time he studied every detail of the house, the location of its front door, its windows, the placement of its chimney, the slant of the roof, the way the big trees crowded up to it from the rear. He could see that certain upstairs windows showed up differently from others in the light of the lowering sun.

When all this information was photographically recorded in his brain, he turned to Julie, smiled suddenly, and said, "Not a twit to be seen."

"What can I do?" Julie asked seriously.

"About what?"

"About tonight. I'm coming along to help."

"No you're not," said the Saint firmly.

"He's *my* brother!" she flared.

"Don't worry," he said, making her stroll at a leisurely pace with him through the woods. "You'll have plenty to do. My object is to get your brother and the Rembrandt safely out of that farmhouse. Then I'll send him to the Golden Fleece, where you'll be waiting for him. You then contact the local police, Adrian can explain how he was kidnapped, and the Dorset constabulary can round up the casualties from the farmhouse."

"Casualties?" she objected. "How do you know *you* won't be a casualty?"

He took her by the arm and steered her back down the hill towards his car.

"Just let me worry about my end of it," he said. "Yours is to be waiting for your brother and call the local cops. But when you call them don't mention Caffin or Pargit."

"Whyever not?"

"I don't want to risk them skinning out. Now listen to this carefully: Get the police to arrange transportation for you and Adrian to London. Tell them there are some urgent angles to this which you'll only discuss with Chief Inspector Teal at Scotland Yard. Then, but only then, when you see him, first thing tomorrow morning, tell him about Pargit and Caffin."

"Why not tell them right away?"

"Because our brave bobbies have been known to bungle and let people escape. I have not."

"Oh," said Julie, and went with him docilely to the car.

CHAPTER 9

Only from very close by was it possible to detect slivers of light at several of the upstairs windows of the old farmhouse. Simon Templar gave no such careless hints of his own presence in that moonless night. In dark clothing, he was one moment a tree trunk, another moment a section of crumbling wall, the next moment an indistinguishable part of the house itself.

Having reached the house after leaving certain equipment at the base of the nearest trees, he made his way soundlessly round the side of the building, and then to the front. The softly chirping night gave no warning sign of the approaching commotion.

The first to feel its impact was one Alfonso "Sleepy" Trocadero, Caffin's most exotic import, who liked napping in the afternoon who was therefore well suited for beginning the first half of the night watch at 10 P.M. If indeed it is accurate to say that Alfonso felt anything. He was sitting stolidly in the darkness behind the locked door of the farmhouse, contemplating the vast vacancies of his moustachioed skull, when there were six knocks— three fast, three slow.

It was the correct signal, and it was proper that it should come at night. There was no telephone at the farmhouse, and messengers, supplies, or reinforcements from London could be expected to arrive in just this way.

Unsuspecting, Alfonso hauled his generously nourished bulk from the chair, turned a key, threw a bolt, and opened the door a little. Seeing no one immediately, he cautiously poked his head outside. It was then that he might have felt something if the light of his nervous system had not been extinguished so suddenly that there was no time even for a signal to race from the back of his neck to his brain.

When he rejoined the world, he was no longer at the still unalarmed farmhouse. He was lying on his back in the woods, looking up at stars beyond the treetops, at the patient face of a man in dark clothing, and at the point of his own flick knife. This eight-inch blade was such a part of his personality that his first automatic reaction was to confirm that his pocket was really empty. But his arm would not move. He was so thoroughly trussed up that he could move nothing but his head, and he did not care to move it when he saw the look in his captor's eyes, which seemed almost to glow in the night.

"Now, friend," the man with the dagger said, "there are certain things I want to hear from you and certain things I don't want to hear. I have very delicate ears, and anything louder than a whisper tends to make me very nervous."

"Who are you?" Alfonso stammered.

The point of the knife moved closer to the tip of his nose.

"I also dislike hearing questions," the other told him. "I like asking them, though, and nothing pleases me more than hearing correct answers. If you tell me something, and I find out you were a naughty boy and didn't tell me the truth, I'm going to give this little toy of yours back to you in a location you won't enjoy. Now, how many people are in that house besides you?"

He pressed the point of the knife against the bulbous end of Alfonso's nose much more gently, he was sure, than Alfonso had used it against his own victims, but firmly enough to produce immediate co-operation.

"Ah—three," said Alfonso.

"Does that include the painter?"

"Painter?"

The knife, which had eased away, renewed its pressure.

"Is there a painter in there? An artist, painting a picture?"

"Yes."

"And two guards besides you?"

"Yes."

The Saint had waited after dropping Alfonso to see if another head would appear at the front door, or if an alarm would be raised. Neither had happened. If the door-guard's absence was discovered, no harm would be done; it might even bring another of Caffin's gang outside to expose himself to the Saint's attentions. Meanwhile, Simon had been able to enter the lower floor of the house and make certain preparations before taking Alfonso off to the woods.

"They're upstairs, right?" Simon continued. "I want to know which window belongs to the room where the painter is."

He propped his captive up against a tree trunk so that he could see the farmhouse and give a detailed description of the arrangements on the second floor. When Simon was satisfied, he dragged the big man farther into the copse and tied him securely to a sapling.

66

"One more question: Is anybody else supposed to come out here tonight?"

"I don't know. Nobody say."

Simon knotted a gag over his prisoner's mouth.

"Okay—why not catch up on your beauty sleep," he suggested. "But if you should feel the temptation to try to make any noise, I want you to know that I'll be the one who'll come and give you a very sharp answer."

"Nng," said Alfonso.

Simon had been intrigued with the possibilities of the farmhouse's chimney ever since he had first started planning his attack. It rose at the end of the house where the trees of the encroaching woods leaned most closely towards the building, had the place been regularly inhabited, no owner would have allowed such intimacies between the branches and his roof. As it was, the trees furnished a perfect means for the Saint to climb to the top of the house. With Adrian a potential hostage inside, he had to avoid any form of assault that might endanger the artist or make him a getaway hostage for his guards.

Simon picked up a knapsack from the ground where he had left it twenty minutes before, and was just easing the straps over his arms when he heard inappropriate sounds in the woods behind him: a stealthy crunching of fallen leaves and twigs, and then suddenly a short sharp cry, gasps, and a thrashing in the copse's dry debris.

The knapsack was instantly back on the ground. The Saint moved as swiftly and silently through the trees as a cloud's shadow. There must be no warning for those in the farmhouse, no use of the pistol in his shoulder holster. In his hand was the switch knife of the man he had captured. He never slowed down. A figure was stumbling from the spot where Simon's captive was tied. A moment later the figure was locked around the throat by an arm as strong and hard as steel, while the dagger promised worse to come.

"Peace, brother," whispered the Saint. "One squawk and you're dead."

Even as he spoke, certain not unpleasant sensations conveyed by the body he was holding told him that he had used the wrong gender.

"Sister?" he corrected.

"Simon?" croaked Julie, as he eased the pressure of his arm on her throat.

"Don't talk out loud!"

"Simon, there's a man there, on the ground! I fell over him."

"I know. I left him there."

Simon then indulged in some colourful comments on the intellectual shortcomings of damsels who should have been left in distress, and what this one thought she was doing here tripping over his playmates in the dark.

"I'm sorry. I wanted to help. I had to know what was happening to you and Adrian."

"What did you do—take a taxi?"

"I borrowed a bicycle. Actually, I stole it from outside the bar, but—"

"I don't have time to hear about it now," Simon told her grimly. "You may be endangering your brother's life. Stay out here; see that this gorilla doesn't get loose or make any noise. Do not panic and run for the police no matter what you think is happening. Wait here for Adrian." She started to open her mouth. "And keep quiet!"

He about-faced and went quickly back to the tree where he had left his knapsack. Moments later he was high up among the branches. For a man of his agility and strength it was simple to use even those unstable and yielding supports to swing to the roof of the house.

His soft-soled shoes made no sound on the slates. He made his way up the gentle incline to the chimney, whose exterior outlines traced a way to a fireplace on the ground floor. First he secured one end of a long rope round the chimney and coiled the remainder at his feet. Then he opened his knapsack and took out a plastic bag containing a sizeable bundle of rags soaked in oil. He spilled gasoline from a small bottle on to some of the rags, ignited them one by one, and dropped them down the chimney.

When a thick column of black smoke began to rise between him and the night sky, he stuffed the knapsack into the chimney's mouth and waited. What could be more alarming to those entrusted with the care of a priceless Rembrandt than the threat of fire? Simon did not think he would have to wait very long.

In about five minutes he heard men's voices coming muffled through the windows just below him. Grasping the rope, he edged down to the rim of the roof.

"Alf? Alf?" someone was shouting.

The time was almost here, and the Saint's timing would have to be perfect. He used the rope in mountain-climber style, using it to support himself as he went down over the eave and leaned out into the darkness with his feet braced against the stone side of the house. The first guard to go down looking for the source of the smoke would hopefully get the full benefit of the surprise that the Saint had set up for him earlier on the stairs . . . a strand of wire stretched just below knee level between the railings and the wall.

"Go look, can't you!" a heavy voice shouted.

The Saint tensed his legs. His ears strained to detect what at last he heard—a distant tumbling succession of thuds far down in the house.

Then he unleashed all the coiled power in his leg-muscles. He sprang out from the side of the house, and swinging in again sailed feet first through the window he had chosen.

All his astonishingly quick perceptions were required to pull together the fragmented impressions that came as he smashed through the window-glass and hurtled into the room where he knew Adrian was held prisoner. Even coming so suddenly from darkness into light, even in the split second of landing on his feet and throwing aside the rope, he saw it all: the big easels to his right, the slight bearded man cowering beside them, the much broader back of another man who was heading for the door of the room as the Saint made his acrobatic entrance.

Even though he had never felt called upon to perform such a feat, Simon might have passed his hand safely beneath the smashing spring of a rat trap between the time it was released and the time it struck home. He moved just as swiftly now. The man at the door was still in the process of spinning round to see what had happened to the window behind him when the Saint struck. There was no need for even a short struggle. The guard's head was simply carried straight and heartily into the wall by the Saint's flying leap. This vigourous encounter of oak and bone produced a most satisfying result, from Simon's point of view at any rate. For his victim it meant instant escape from all worldly cares and responsibilities, at least until he woke up with a mild concussion some hours later.

As he drew his automatic, Simon said soothingly to the frightened young man on his right, "I'm here to help you. Don't move. Don't do anything. Just tell me, how many guards are here with you tonight?"

"Three, I think."

Satisfied that his first captive had told the truth, Simon switched off the light and moved into the corridor. He could make out the head of the stairway by a dim strip of light which escaped through the door of another room. The air was heavy with smoke. He heard a groan below.

"If you are awake," he called cheerfully, "don't move or I will shoot you dead."

Apparently a groan was about all that the man at the foot of the stairs was capable of. Simon could see that he was sprawled awkwardly, with his right arm at an unnatural angle, broken or thrown out of joint by his crash. With his pistol aimed at the injured man's head, Simon went down the steps and made him secure, if not more comfortable, with the same piece of wire which had caused his downfall.

Back in Norcombe's room with the light again, Simon had his

first good look at the young artist. Long brown hair and beard wreathed his countenance so that he looked like a gnome peering out of a bird's nest. He was very pale, probably more so on this occasion than usual; his long boney hands fluttered apprehensively as he watched the unconscious man on the floor being tied hand and foot.

"My name is Simon Templar," the Saint introduced himself, rising to lounge easily on the arm of a chair, with his automatic back in its holster. "I've come to get you out of this mess. Your sister's outside waiting for you."

"Julie!" Adrian exclaimed eagerly. "Is she all right? They told me if I didn't do what they wanted they'd do dreadful things to her."

"She's fine. How about you?"

"I'm all right. Are you the police?"

"No, I'm just a friend. Julie knows what you're supposed to do now, while I finish rounding up the rest of this gang. I'm going to leave you with her, and you do exactly what she says. She can explain everything."

Simon walked over to the two easels, admiringly compared the original with Adrian's almost completed imitation, and took the true Rembrandt off its supports.

"This will go back to its owner," he told Adrian. "Now come on downstairs."

"Is the house on fire?" Adrian queried, as he followed.

"No. That was just a smoke-screen."

Simon shepherded the artist out the front door of the house, and then came one of those vaguely foreseeable but unpredictable things which can give the agley treatment to the best-laid plans of mice. But not necessarily of men—or some men. The lights of a car appeared on the narrow road leading in towards the house.

"Run!" snapped the Saint, giving Adrian a shove. "Straight back there—you'll find Julie about a hundred yards into the woods. Don't either of you wait or come near here again!"

Adrian did not need urging. He sprinted away towards the frontier of trees with surprising speed. Simon spun round and dashed back into the house, closing the door behind him just as the automobile's lights swept full across the roof of the old well. He put the painting safely aside, wished he had time to douse the smouldering rags which were filling the place with smoke, drew his automatic again, and stood behind the bolted door.

Footsteps. One man's footsteps. Then six knocks in the password pattern. Smoothly the Saint freed the latch and opened the door, keeping his face in the darkness.

"My God, is the place on fire?" cried the man on the threshold.

The Saint felt one of those moments of supreme satisfaction which helped make his adventures worthwhile from much more than a financial point of view.

"No, indeed, Mr. Pargit-Fawkes. Just a little something I was cooking up. As a matter of fact, everything is under perfect control." He then confronted the art dealer with his pistol in a manner that caused Pargit's refined hands to rise directly into the air like a pair of hoisted flags. "But in view of the uncomfortable conditions here, I'd be much obliged if you could drive me in to London. I'd like us to pay a call together on a colleague of yours."

CHAPTER 10

Chief Inspector Claud Eustace Teal arrived at his Scotland Yard office at 9:35 in the morning to discover that others than the Lord move in mysterious ways, and that the axiom about His helping those who help themselves occasionally makes an exception for those whose minds are on other things entirely.

Not that Teal had completely forgotten Templar and their mysteriously abbreviated visit to the Leonardo Galleries, but he would hardly have associated it at first with the mystery that greeted him when he walked into his Spartan chambers. Before he could be told the business of the bearded young man and slender girl who waited in his ante-room, a telephone was thrust into his plump hand, and the voice of his superior, the Assistant Commissioner, came through in tones startlingly lacking their habitual acerbity.

"Teal, I must congratulate you! A good job. I've just had a call from Lord Oldenshaw on the return of his painting. He's pleased as Punch, which isn't surprising, considering the thing turns out to be worth half a million. Have you been back in touch with the Dorset police this morning?"

Mr Teal was beginning to exhibit the symptoms of any unemployed handyman who has just been informed that he has been awarded the Nobel Prize for Physics.

"Not yet," he improvised. "I wanted to get a few more details sorted out first—"

"They're holding the three for us in Dorset until we decide if we want them here," the Assistant Commissioner informed him. "Lord Oldenshaw was under the impression you'd be rounding up the ringleaders here in London. What are you doing about it?"

"I . . . I'm setting it up now," Teal said. "It's a ticklish business. I've got to be sure there aren't any loose ends."

"Carry on!" the Assistant Commissioner said. "Report back to me as soon as you can, and the best of British luck."

Chief Inspector Teal, trying feverishly to fathom his chief's unwonted cordiality, hung up the telephone and shakily stuffed a stick of spearmint into his mouth. His cherubic countenance glistened, moist and red. Through his brain hurtled awful fantasies of some Saintish prank that would make him, earnest and hardworking Chief Inspector Teal, the immortal dunce of Scotland Yard.

"What happened in Dorset?" he asked his secretary, keeping his voice low.

"The Norcombes notified the local police where they could pick up the gang who'd been holding Mr. Norcombe a prisoner."

"Norcombes?" Teal said blankly.

"Those are the Norcombes, waiting to see you."

Teal decided wisely that the less he said the less his ignorance would become manifest to the world. He went out again into the ante-room.

"Mr and Mrs Norcombe?"

"Not Mr and Mrs," the girl replied. "I'm Julie Norcombe. This is my brother, Adrian."

Adrian jumped to his feet and stuck out his hand. Teal shook it warily.

"Would you come into my office, please?" he said.

In that sanctuary he soon heard the whole story, in which the names of Caffin, Pargit, and Templar were frequently involved. It was a story that was almost complete: Adrian rescued from his kidnappers, the genuine Rembrandt revealed as genuine and already returned to a delighted Lord Oldenshaw. The only thing that remained undone was the capture of the leaders.

Teal was goaded out of his normal passivity by the challenge. The Saint had already done most of the work singlehanded. Hours had passed. If the masterminds of the plot escaped, Teal would feel the barbs of his failure for ever each time he saw Simon Templar's mocking grin.

"Thank you very much Mr Norcombe, Miss Norcombe. You'll be taken care of here until we finish this job. My secretary will take your statements in writing, and of course we'll need you for purposes of identification. Would you please wait outside a little longer?"

He sat at his desk and proceeded to set wheels in motion with what for him was a positive frenzy of momentum. There would be simultaneous raids on Caffin's and Pargit's residences, as well as the Leonardo Galleries. A subordinate was sent post-haste to obtain search warrants. Pargit, being a softer type of crook and less organised, could be expected to fall most easily into the hands of the police. Caffin, a known gang boss, would get Teal's personal attention. Caffin's flat had been under surveillance before for various reasons, and a Flying Squad car was despatched to cover the known exits and verify his presence until Teal could arrive on the scene.

As soon as he knew that all the cogs in his machinery were meshing smoothly, Teal left his office by another door, settled his bowler hat on his perspiring head, and clomped downstairs to the unmarked car that he had ordered to wait for him.

Although he could never have been called loquacious, his cohorts had seldom seen him so muted by his own tension. The detective-sergeant driver had to remind him that he had yet to give them their destination.

"We're going to pick up Sam Caffin," Teal said rigidly, and added a scrap of fingernail to the gum he was chewing.

"Caffin," the sergeant repeated cautiously.

"Sam Caffin. You know him and where he lives."

"Yes, sir," said the sergeant, and decided it would be wiser not to ask any more questions.

A plainclothes man in overalls, on a ladder, was assiduously fiddling with a street-lamp near Caffin's apartment building when Teal's equally unofficial-looking car parked near by. As Teal got out, the lamp-fiddler paused in his labours to pull out a green handkerchief and blow his nose, signalling that all instructions had been carried out. If there had been problems, the handkerchief, from another pocket, would have been white, asking for a discreet conference.

A husky young constable, in unobtrusively casual clothes, followed Teal into the building and towards the elevator. As they reached it, it discharged a stout matron and her poodle, and Teal noted with satisfaction that they were met at the street door and engaged on some pretext by his sergeant driver—a routine precaution against any of the intended objectives slipping through the cordon in disguise, improbable as that particular transmogrification might have seemed.

As the lift bore him and his junior colleague to Caffin's floor, Teal clutched and turned his bowler like a racing driver manipulating the wheel of his car as he steered through a final chicane.

They arrived, uneventfully, at Caffin's door. Teal knocked, wishfully hoping that it would be Caffin himself who looked out at him when the door opened—assuming that it was opened without resistance. In spite of all precautions, there was always a risk, with a man like Caffin, that some leak might have sprung an unforeseen weakness in the trap.

The door did open, but it was not the beefy countenance of Sam Caffin which met Chief Inspector Teal's consternated stare.

He should long since have accustomed himself to these experiences, but somehow he never did. When he was confronted by the suave and smiling face of Simon Templar, he felt as if the entire building had suddenly evaporated, leaving him standing precariously fifty feet up in the air.

"Scotland Yard, I presume?" said the Saint, stepping back to let them enter. He was wearing a strangely formal outfit consisting of immaculate dark coat and striped trousers. "I'm afraid you've missed the party, but we still have some leftovers."

When Teal entered, in a kind of ponderous daze, he saw that the leftovers consisted of Caffin, Pargit, and another man, sitting in a neat row on the sofa, arms and legs tied. Two small revolvers lay on the coffee table in front of them. With wildly disarrayed hair, rumpled clothing, and bruised faces, the trio looked like the survivors of a tornado.

"Boys," said the Saint, "meet Chief Inspector Claud Eustace Teal of Scotland Yard. With his usual prompt efficiency, he's arrived to take you away. You're going to be having some long chats with him, so you might as well start getting acquainted. As for me, I'll just be bumbling off. It was nice meeting you."

He was on his way out when Teal caught up with him and followed him into the corridor outside the flat.

"Hold up there, Templar," he commanded. "You're not getting out of here without some explanations. I've got this place surrounded."

"I'm overwhelmed by your gratitude," Simon said humbly.

Teal calmed down a little. He tried to control his burning envy of this man who seemed to do more alone—defying the laws—than Teal could do with the whole of Scotland Yard behind him.

"It's not that I don't appreciate the way this has turned out," the detective said, and for him that was a great and noble admission. "But what happened here? What are you doing in that suit?"

"Ah, the suit. Mr Pargit was kind enough to give me a lift to London and bring me calling on his friend Caffin. But I wasn't sure that Caffin would be so polite if I introduced myself as the notorious Saint, so I decided to seek an audience with him as an Inland Revenue man. The fact that Pargit and I happened to come up the lift at the same time would be sheer coincidence. I got in quite easily. For some inexplicable reason nobody ever seems to think of shooting an income-tax inspector."

"And so you beat them all up singlehanded."

The Saint's eyebrows lifted innocently.

"They weren't beat up. We just had what are known in diplomatic circles as frank and productive discussions. A vigourous bargaining session. It was really Pargit's fault. He's a born haggler." Simon lounged against the corridor wall with exasperating nonchalance, looking as if he had just emerged from a session with his tailor rather than two thugs and an art shark. "Remember that old lady I told you about—the one Pargit took for a sucker when he sold her an eighth-rate painting for several times what is was worth? I was here as her representative. Pargit was reluctant to make restitution at first, but we talked it over at length and he finally saw the error of his ways. I have his personal check for the dear old dame. Even though he's repented, I suppose it's too late to keep him out of jail, but I'm sure his soul will benefit enormously."

"Templar," Teal smouldered. "All I can say is . . ."

And, in fact, that was absolutely all he could say.

That evening, Simon entertained Julie and Adrian Norcombe at one of London's quieter and more admirable restaurants.

While sole and duck underwent awesome transformations from their natural state, in a kitchen far removed from the crystal and candlelight of the dining room, the Saint raised his first glass of Bollinger.

"Dearly beloved," he said, "we are gathered here not only to celebrate Adrian's freedom and the general triumph of justice, but also something a little more tangible. Let's drink to all three."

When they had sipped, Adrian put forward his own glass and said shyly, "Thank you."

He and his sister toasted the Saint. And Julie asked, "Tangible?"

Simon settled back in his chair, pulled a slip of tinted paper from his coat pocket, and placed it on the table in front of them. They studied its simple but eloquent words and numerals, and stared at him in astonishment.

"Ten thousand pounds?" Julie quoted hoarsely.

"For you to divide between you," Simon said.

"But why should you write us a check like that?" she objected.

"I wrote the check, but the money isn't from me," Simon told her. "When I told Lord Oldenshaw that the painting he'd given Pargit was a true and actual Rembrandt, and that we'd saved it from being hijacked, and that I could return it to him immediately, he was so anxious to get his hands on it that he could hardly wait to show his gratitude. Fifteen thousand pounds' worth. A small enough cut out of the half a million or more he'll get for the painting if he decides to sell it. Of course if the experts he's no doubt got swarming all over the painting tell him it *isn't* a genuine Rembrandt, the check he gave me won't be worth tuppence in the morning. It *is* genuine, isn't it, Adrian?"

He said it mainly to draw Adrian out. The young man had so far proved incapable of putting more than three words together consecutively.

"Oh, I'm certain it is. And Mr Pargit must have been sure it was or he wouldn't have gone to all that trouble."

Julie impulsively reached out and touched the Saint's hand.

"Simon, it was wonderful of you to do this."

Since Simon could only agree, he simply smiled and quietly appreciated the lingering warmth of her fingers. Adrian was obviously struggling to organise a new sentence.

"I . . . I'm very grateful," he said. "Perhaps I could show it by doing a painting for you. Whom would you prefer?"

"Whom?" the Saint asked.

"Which artist?"

"Why, you, Adrian. You have money in the bank, now. You can afford to do your own work."

"I'm afraid my only talent is imitating," Adrian said resignedly. "Would you like a—an El Greco?"

"Something soothing," the Saint proposed. "Gainsborough."

Adrian beamed.

"Oh, good. I haven't tried Gainsborough."

"You've got a model in the family."

Julie rested her chin in her hand and looked pensively at the Saint.

"I wish I had a talent, so I could show my gratitude."

"I'm sure you'll think of something," Simon responded. "For a start you could keep me company when I go back to Dorset to pick up my car. We might even find time to do a little bird-watching."

She brightened.

"Oh, I'd love that." Then, for his eyes alone, her mouth formed the word she had said she would never say to him: *"Darling."*

The Adoring Socialite

CHAPTER 1

In the course of his good works, of which he himself was not the smallest beneficiary, the man so paradoxically called the Saint had assumed many roles and placed himself in such a fantastic variety of settings that the adventures of a Sinbad or a Ulysses had by comparison all the excitement of a housewife's trip to the market. His range was the world. His identities had encompassed cowboy and playboy, poet and revolutionary, hobo and millionaire. The booty he had gathered in his years of buccaneering had certainly made the last category genuine: The assets he had salted away would have made headlines if they had been exposed to counting. He could have comfortably retired at an age when most men are still angling for their second promotion. But strong as the profit motive was as a factor in his exploits, there were other drives which would never allow him to put the gears of his mind permanently in neutral and hang up his heels on the stern rail of a yacht. He had an insatiable lust for action, in a world that squandered its energies on speeches and account books. He craved the individual expression of his own personal ideals, and his rules were not those of parliaments and judges but those of a man impatient to accomplish his purposes, according to his own lights, by the most effective means available at the moment.

This does not mean that all his waking hours were consecrated to one clear-cut objective or another, attached to which there had to be the eventual prospect of some pecuniary reward. Like anyone else, he often found himself enmeshed in quite aimless activities, some of which promised nothing but entries on the debit side of his imaginary ledgers.

Like, for instance, this very Main-Line charity ball in Philadelphia, for which the tickets cost a mere $100 each against the $1,000 that many social climbers would have paid to get one. In a situation that has nothing to do with this story, Simon Templar had been offered the ineffable privilege of buying one at cost, as a favour that he could not gracefully refuse; and since he had paid his money and had nothing more exciting on his agenda at the moment, he had decided that he might as well look in, in a spirit of scientific if not wholly unmalicious curiosity, and see what cooked in this particular segment of the Upper Crust.

It was an impulse for which his first impression was that he should have had his head examined. The Adelphi Ballroom of the New Sylvania Hotel was like a claustrophobic football field thronged with players attempting to get champagne glasses from one point to another without splashing the contents over themselves or their neighbours or being toppled by dancers encroaching on drinkers' territory. The air was dense with the essence of acres of French flowers and the effluvium of smouldering tobacco leaves. Words were lost in a whirlpool of words. Individuality was swallowed up in the mass.

The Saint stood observing the scene cynically, restless, his mind in other places, like a privateer waiting for the tide that would set him free from the shore. When a plump warm hand touched his wrist it was no surprise, even though he had given no sign of anticipating it; his life had depended so frequently on his instincts that even in surroundings as apparently safe as these, even with his mind abstracted, it would have been virtually impossible for anyone to approach him from any direction without his being aware of it well in advance of arrival.

But he looked down into the doughy pink unity that constituted the face and chins of Miss Theresa Marpeldon as if her fragrant advent had been a complete surprise. He had met her once, briefly and unmemorably, at a cocktail party in Palm Beach. Miss Theresa Marpeldon was about seventy, and the heiress of a baked-bean fortune. She was heavily powdered, soaked in cologne, and wreathed in diamonds for this occasion. In the Saint's imagination she resembled the decorative pudding of some baronial Christmas banquet.

"Simon," she said, "there's a young lady here who's dying to meet you."

"I already like her," the Saint said amiably. "Who is she?"

"She's right here. She *was* right here. Carole?"

Miss Marpeldon kept a precautionary hold on the Saint's arm as she turned to look for her protégé.

From behind she was all beautiful young legs and long blond hair. When Miss Marpeldon turned her round, the Saint began to feel that he was getting value for his hundred dollars. She was in her twenties, with a pert Scottish nose and wide turquoise eyes. There were many decorative women in the room, but this girl stood out like a single flower in a field of grass. The turquoise eyes met the deep blue of the Saint's with level playfulness.

"Carole, I was just telling Mr Templar that you were dying to meet him, and then you wandered off."

"I never said I was dying to meet you," the girl denied. "All I said was that if Theresa didn't introduce us I was going to hang myself from that chandelier during the last waltz."

Miss Marpeldon giggled loudly, like any good audience for society-ballroom wit.

"This is Carole Angelworth," she said. "Carole, this is Simon Templar. I'm sure you two can find plenty to talk about."

Miss Marpeldon was a born matchmaker, and was immediately off to the rescue of a gangly young man whose very costly tuxedo seemed to be doing him no good at all in his search for a dancing partner.

"I'm flattered that you were considering suicide over me before we'd even met," Simon said to Carole Angelworth. "It's understandable, but still flattering."

"Oh, think nothing of it," she replied airily. "I've told her the same thing about at least two other men this evening."

"What happened to them?"

"Appearances can be deceiving. They just didn't live up to their looks." She paused and shrugged. "So I poisoned them."

"Naturally," the Saint nodded. "I have a feeling I'll be safer if your hands are occupied. Let's dance."

"Well, normally I dance with my feet, but I'll see what I can do."

"Much more of that corn and I might poison *you*," Simon warned her.

She slipped easily into his arms, and they merged with the other dancers in a slow old-fashioned fox trot, or rather a sort of intimate shuffle, which was about as much movement as the crowded floor allowed. Something in the way her hand held his belied the cool banter of her gilt-edged accent. Before he had ever seen her, she had been watching him. Among the other younger males in the ballroom—who were generally over-fed, over-protected, and under-exercised—Simon Templar's lean tall strength and almost sinister handsomeness had attracted her immediately. Now, as she danced close to him, his magnetism captured her even more, and she found it hard to breathe.

"I don't know that much about you," she said with an effort at her original nonchalance. "Do you really and truly think we ought to run away together?"

"Give me another half minute to think it over," Simon said.

She leaned back a little and looked up at him.

"Who are you?" she asked. "I've never seen you at one of these brawls before."

"I move round a lot," he told her.

"Where?"

"Wherever my business takes me."

"What's your business?"

"It varies," he said. "Mostly armed robbery, jewel thieving, large-scale swindles."

"I knew you were the kind of man who wouldn't tell anything about himself. You like being mysterious."

"At least I've said something," Simon replied. "What about you?"

"My name is Carole Angelworth," she recited with her eyes closed. "I am twenty-three years old. I have a degree in sociology. My mother is dead. I live with my father, Hyram J. Angelworth, who is very rich and generous, and spoils me rotten. I am reasonably normal except for a mad urge to climb trees just before the full moon. I have a passion for back-rubs and strawberries."

"At least back-rubs are never out of season," Simon mused. "But then, I suppose neither are strawberries, when your father is Hyram J. Angelworth."

"You've heard of him?" Carole asked.

The music ended just then, and they strolled towards one of the bars.

"You can't be in Philadelphia long without hearing about him. The Angelworth Foundation. The Angelworth Children's Clinic. The Citizens Committee for Law Enforcement. He's done the town a lot of good."

"He's a good man," Carole said earnestly. "Sometimes I'm afraid people take advantage of him. He worked hard for what he's got, and now he gives it away right and left. You don't even know a fraction of the things he does—the charities. But I hate that word. It sounds so condescending."

"Well, there are worse ways for a man to get his kicks," said the Saint. "And from the looks of that solid-silver dress of yours, he's at least keeping enough cash round to pay the light bills."

"It's rude to comment on the price of things," Carole remarked.

"Whoever said I wasn't rude?" Simon retorted.

Once they had met, there was no question of their parting. Simon could see that behind her bantering façade, she really had developed an instant crush on him; and he would have been less than human if he had not responded to her dew-fresh beauty and youthful exuberance. They spent the evening happily together. Carole turned down several requests to dance with other men. It was only when the ball had rolled beyond its midnight peak that she and Simon were surrounded by half a dozen of her friends insisting that they all go off together to a livelier spot. Simon left it up to Carole, who had no particular fondness for the overpowering elegance of the ballroom.

"Go ahead, and we'll meet you there," she told the other couples. "I want to tell Daddy good night and introduce him to Simon."

He was mildly surprised when, at the elevators, she pressed an UP button.

"We live here," she explained. "In the penthouse apartment. Daddy glommed on to it when the hotel was being built."

"I've always wanted to see how the under-privileged people make out," he murmured.

"Where are you staying?"

"Here, too, as a matter of fact. But not in quite such grandeur. I took a room here because the ball was here and it seemed to save a lot of running about, and because they have a garage in the basement."

"So you don't mind a few modern comforts either."

She found her father in a book-lined library off the formal drawing room, sitting in leather-upholstered comfort with three guests of about his own age and a considerably younger fourth —a tall hunched man with long arms and a watchful pair of ball-bearing eyes deeply imbedded under dark bushy brows—

standing behind him. *Bodyguard?* Simon immediately asked himself, for the standing man's face would have seemed more at home on a post-office wall than here in the company of the thoroughbred rich.

"Daddy, this is Mr Templar. He's been taking beautiful care of your only daughter all evening, so I thought you'd like to express your gratitude." She turned to Simon. "Daddy's always petrified I'm going to fall in with evil companions, or be kidnapped or something."

Angelworth put down his liqueur and rose from his green wing-backed chair to shake hands. He combined an air of command with a natural modesty which made him both impressive and likeable at first sight. He was in his late fifties, almost as tall as the Saint, with a carefully tended mane of white hair which contributed to making his head seem larger than the heads of the people around him. His mouth was broad and strong, but softened into an almost benign smile.

"If you've been making my daughter's life happier I'm particularly pleased to meet you," he said.

"And I'm particularly pleased to meet the father of the young lady who's given me such a delightful evening," Simon replied with equal graciousness.

The names of the others, punctiliously introduced, would have needed no references from Dun & Bradstreet, with the exception of the craggy-browed fourth, whose name was Richard Hamlin and whose handshake and grunt were as short on urbanity as his appearance.

"My secretary and aide-de-camp," Angelworth explained.

Carole surveyed the other three suspiciously.

"You string-pullers aren't still trying to talk my father into running for governor, are you?"

Hyram Angelworth sat down with a weary smile.

"I'm afraid that's what they've been trying to do," he said.

"Well, you just leave him alone," Carole said. "He doesn't need all those dirty politics, and he's doing plenty of good just as he is."

"Can't promise you that," one of the men said. "We need him. There aren't many born winners round these days."

Angelworth raised a hand.

"Don't worry, dear," he said to Carole, "the answer will go right on being no. I'm better as a gadfly than a demagogue."

"As long as that's understood," his daughter said with mock sharpness, "Simon and I can leave you to take care of yourself. The gang's going out for a little hot jazz. I'll be home in a couple of hours."

Her father said good-bye in a barely perceptible tone of resignation, like a would-be disciplinarian who has long ago given up on a recalcitrant subject.

"You notice," Carole murmured to Simon when they were out of earshot, "that I didn't say we were going *with* the gang."

"Oh? Do you have a different plan?"

"I don't need all that noise tonight any more than my father needs to hornswoggle the masses into giving him the honour of having mud slung at him for four years. Let's just find a quiet dump where we won't be noticed and have a cup of coffee. It isn't every day I meet somebody interesting enough to bother talking to."

"What, in these rags?"

"After that second crack, I'll change into something less gaudy. You do the same, and I'll meet you in the garage in ten minutes. And I do mean ten minutes."

It was not extraordinary that a girl with the background of Carole Angelworth should have had no inkling that any night out with him had a built-in risk of getting involved with more exciting, and more dangerous, things than talk.

CHAPTER 2

He would have bet that to a girl of her type "ten minutes" was only a figure of speech which might have covered any period up to a half or three quarters of an hour. But she was precisely as good as her word, having simply shucked the low-cut silver lamé creation in exchange for a plain sweater and skirt, in the same time as he had swapped his tuxedo for a jacket and slacks.

His knowledge of Philadelphia geography was minimal, and he let her direct him through rain-wet streets for something over twenty minutes in a direction that began well enough but became progressively more sordid, until they turned a corner close to some pretzels of garish red neon a little down the block which proclaimed the exotic ambience of SAMMY'S BOOZE & BILLIARDS.

Carole pointed.

"Let's go in there."

Simon's brows slanted in a half rise, half frown. But he slowed up and pulled over to the kerb, not directly under the twisted neon but not many yards beyond. As they passed, he observed that to enhance the inspired title of the place there was an ornamental drunk sleeping propped up beside the entrance.

At that hour there was hardly any traffic, and finding parking space was not the problem.

"It looks delightful," Simon said, "but I thought we were hunting for some place quiet and cosy."

"I love slumming," Carole said. She suddenly snuggled up against him and looked up fiendishly into his eyes. "You're not scared to take me in there, are you?"

"I'm sure you'll protect me," Simon drawled. "On the other hand, I'm sure you must know a place or two that might be a little more romantic."

"I've never felt more romantic in my life," Carole insisted. "And I can't imagine anything that would bore me more than one of those conventional all-night supper clubs."

And so, against his better judgement, Simon Templar found himself escorting Carole Angelworth into Sammy's Booze & Billiards on a particular night at a particular time, which proved once again that even in his most off-guard and idle moments the Saint could not escape the currents of destiny that sucked him involuntarily into adventure.

They tiptoed around the sloshed Cerberus couched beside the

threshold, opened the door, and faced the dense dark atmosphere like a pair of divers suddenly plunged into a gloomy pond.

It soon became moderately clear that there was a bar with stools down to the right, booths along the wall paralleling it, and in a larger space to the left a pair of pool tables occupying the earnest attention of several men. Sammy's pool-playing clientele varied from flashily over-dressed to shirt-sleeves and khakis. The trio at the nearest table fell into the flashy category—quick money, low taste. Simon would normally have regarded them as part of the furniture, but he hesitated and looked at one of them again. A look of slightly puzzled concentration came over his face, tentative recognition mixed with uncertainty.

The Saint's brain had a fantastic capacity for keeping vast quantities of stored information available for conscious recall. Thousands of faces, names, aliases, and case histories swarmed beneath the surface of his everyday awareness, ready to be netted and re-examined on an instant's notice. The very fact that Simon hesitated at all after spotting a face that looked vaguely familiar meant that the identity belonging to the face had never played an important part in his own experience. But Simon's natural inquisitiveness, and his dislike of unsolved puzzles, kept him standing just inside the entrance until seconds later an invisible index flipped over in his head and matched the face. Just a name, with an undefined favourable feeling attached to it, but enough to make the Saint impulsively take Carole's arm and step over to the pool table.

"Brad Ryner," he said.

There had been a lull in the game, and the man to whom he spoke looked up from chalking his cue. The look was not one of friendly recognition, or even of ready interest. The other's face—broken-nosed, ruddy, rough-skinned, surmounted by curly red hair—was immediately hostile.

"Who're you talking to?" he asked angrily.

When confronted with animosity, the Saint's self-imposed discipline was to relax rather than to let himself get nettled.

"To you," he said easily. "Aren't you Brad Ryner?"

"No, I'm not, and I never heard of him." Fingers gripped the billiard cue so tightly that knuckles were white. "You've got your wires crossed, buster. The name's Joe, and I don't like people interrupting me when I'm trying to concentrate on a game."

If Carole had known more about Simon Templar, she would have realised that his response was uncharacteristically apologetic.

"Sorry," he said. "I made a mistake."

"Okay, okay!" the other man snarled. "Do me a favour and cut out the yapping or you're gonna wreck my concentration."

His two companions at the table were watching him and the Saint with more interest now than at the beginning. One was a stout, bald, seal-like character with chocolate-coloured eyes and very small ears. The other had the build of a professional football tackle, but the unhealthy pallour of his skin hinted that not many of his activities took place out of doors. He scratched the back of his neck as he studied the face of the man Simon had called Brad Ryner.

Simon took Carole by the arm and moved away from the pool table.

"Nice friends you have," Carole said in a loud voice. "Or non-friends."

"Never mind," the Saint said firmly, steering her to a booth at the other end of the bar. "You picked the place, so you shouldn't be surprised to meet down-to-earth types. Or did you expect we'd be recognised and given the V.I.P. treatment?"

"That comes very close to sounding snide."

"Nothing snide intended," Simon said abstractedly. As he slipped into the dark booth next to the girl he could see that the three pool players had resumed their game. "I just pulled a boner, and I'm annoyed with myself."

Carole shrugged.

"Well, anybody could mistake a face in this light, so don't let it spoil our evening."

"I won't if you won't."

The unshaven shirt-sleeved counterman came and took their order for coffee.

"I still don't see why he had to be so rude," Carole said while they waited. "Or why you let him get away with it."

"Forget it," Simon answered. "I don't want to talk about it here."

They never did recapture the playfulness and gaiety of the earlier part of the evening. Simon parried Carole's questions about his own life by drawing her out about her own. It had been a sheltered existence. Her mother had died while Carole was still a child. She had been nurtured by nannies, maids, and governesses. Her teens had unfolded trivially in a setting of sail-boats, tennis, house-parties, and debutante balls. Self-mocking, she described herself as a violet blossoming in the shade of a great oak.

The great oak was her father. He had not had her advantages when he was young, and typically he had tried to insulate her from the harsh realities which he had overcome.

"So it was rags to riches," Simon prompted her, thinking how refreshing it was in these days to meet a rich girl who so positively and genuinely admired and adored the parent whose upward struggle had given her so much.

"Well, not exactly rags," Carole replied. "Just the ordinary lower-middle-class slog, cutting corners and keeping a beady eye on the budget. Until he struck it rich when I was going to college. I was a spoiled brat, and for a long time I just rebelled against him, but I've finally gotten old enough to appreciate what he's done. I can even admit how proud I am of him. When you have time, I'd like to show you a couple of places he's responsible for creating."

She turned her thick coffee-cup in its stained saucer and frowned slightly.

"Of course sometimes he goes too far. You'd think from all his law-and-order talk, and what a hardheaded businessman he is, that he'd be more careful. But he's a great one for rehabilitating people—like that Richard Hamlin you met tonight. Richard's an ex-convict. Embezzlement and who knows what else. But Daddy took him under his wing and made him his personal secretary."

"Hire the handicapped, huh? I thought the casting director had done an off-beat job including Hamlin in that group. Still, he must have a fair set of brains. Embellishing books can be a fine art."

"Oh, I don't think he's dumb," Carole said. "I just don't trust him."

"Why?" he asked with new interest.

But her dislike of Hamlin turned out to be based more on instinctive prejudice and unconscious snobbery (and perhaps a little jealousy of the secretary's close and confidential relationship with her father) than on facts. It was a prejudice that many a wife has indulged—and usually denied—against the other woman in her husband's office.

"Helping a lame dog over a stile is supposed to be good boy-scout Christianity," Simon remarked judiciously. "Although personally I've always thought it was one of the silliest precepts ever coined. Did you ever look at a stile? I never saw one yet that a lame dog couldn't wriggle over much faster than you could lift him over it."

"Are you being symbolic or just smart?"

"Could be either."

"I suppose you don't believe in women's intuition."

"I pass."

She caught Simon glancing at his watch.

"Am I boring you?" she enquired with some acidity.

"No, you're not, but if you've finished your coffee I'd like to get out of here."

Her reply was to push her empty cup away and pick up her bag from the seat beside her. As he walked with her to the door, Simon noted that the same groups were round the pool tables, and that the seal and the football tackle watched him as he left the bar.

Carole slumped disconsolately as he drove her back towards the New Sylvania.

"We were having such a good time," she pouted. "What's wrong? Did I say something? Are you just upset because you thought that man back there was somebody you knew?"

Seeing her stripped of her protective irony, admitting that her relationship with him meant enough to depress her, Simon felt that he owed her an honest answer.

"All right," he said. "I'll tell you. It has nothing to do with you, and I don't think you could bore me if you recited the telephone directory. I'm still kicking myself because of that imbecilic thing I did back in that bar."

"What's imbecilic about mistaken identity?" she demanded. "I'm surprised a man like you would worry about a thing like that. Male vanity?"

"It wasn't a case of mistaken identity," said the Saint. "It was a case of the mouth outrunning the brain. That man I spoke to really is named Brad Ryner. At least he was a couple of years ago when I met him out in California. And since he had a wife named Doris Ryner, and three kids with the same surname, I don't think I need his birth certificate to prove the point."

"Then why did he say his name was Joe?"

"Because Brad Ryner is a cop. A detective. Figure it out for yourself."

Carole pondered, then said: "I think it would be faster if you explained it to me."

The muscles of his face were tense.

"I'm afraid that Brad Ryner is involved in some kind of under-cover job, using a phoney name, Joe Something, and I just walked in and possibly blew the whole thing for him."

"You mean he's collecting information or something for the police?"

"Yes, and because I spilled the beans he may end up collecting bullets in the back."

"Well," Carole said, "I wouldn't necessarily call it spilling the beans. Even if he was infiltrating a gang, or whatever he's doing, how would the crooks know that somebody named Brad Ryner was a detective?"

"I'm hoping they won't," Simon said. "Ryner had a routine job in a fairly small town on the other side of the continent. There's no reason anybody in Philadelphia should ever have heard his name."

Carole put a hand on Simon's shoulder and smiled.

"Then it wasn't quite like walking in and saying, 'Well, Sherlock Holmes, as I live and breathe!'"

"Not quite," he admitted. "But I'm worried that I might have done just enough to rouse somebody's suspicions, and make them start checking out the name Ryner. Eventually that could mean real trouble."

"At least he's warned," she said. "I mean, before anybody can find out that Brad Ryner is a cop he can get out of the picture."

"And that's my contribution to law and order," said the Saint grimly.

"I'll bet nobody thought a thing about it after we went and sat down," Carole asserted. "They've forgotten the whole thing by now."

"I hope so."

She sensed his lack of conviction, but did not pursue it.

"We're almost there," she said. "Would you like to come up for a nightcap?"

"I'd enjoy it, but we've had a pretty full evening." His concern for Brad Ryner showed clearly in his face and his voice. "Maybe another time."

"I won't chain myself to your bumper if you'll promise to see me tomorrow. Here's my private phone number."

As Simon pulled his car to a halt in the garage, Carole scribbled the number on a scrap of paper from her handbag and gave it to him. Simon went with her as far as the elevator.

"Well?" she said.

"Well?" Simon echoed.

Carole leaned against the wall next to the elevator buttons.

"Well, are you going to go out with me tomorrow, and well, are you going to kiss me good night?"

"Keep it up and you'll make drill sergeant."

"Would you rather I used womanly wiles? I'm just telling you what I want. You don't have to do either one."

Simon's mind jumped forward over the next couple of days. He had no binding plans.

"I think I'll do both," he said.

He bent down and softly kissed her parted lips.

"I'll have to phone you tomorrow about getting together," he told her.

She was looking into his eyes with such melting adoration that he felt uncomfortable about having kissed her. She had asked for it, but apparently there was a very susceptible, child-like female just below that bold and mischievous surface. The elevator doors slid soundlessly open, and Simon shepherded her gently into the mahogany and brass of the cabin.

"Why aren't you riding up too?" she asked.

"I didn't park the car very tidily," he said.

She seemed to come back to earth suddenly.

"You're not going back to that bar, are you?"

"I'd much rather go to bed," he said deviously. "Thanks for a wonderful evening."

She felt an urge to reach for his hand and keep him there, to protect him from the danger she sensed was waiting for him out in the night, but he had stepped back from the elevator, and the doors moved between them. She was alone in a costly cocoon, as she had been during so much of her life, and then she was rising smoothly by virtue of some unseen mechanism to a roost high above the noise and grime of city streets.

She found her father in the living-room of the penthouse, relaxing in purple silk pajamas and dressing gown as he sipped a brandy. His white hair was neatly brushed as always, but his eyes were weary.

Carole kissed him on the cheek.

"I'll bet you're waiting up for me. You're really incorrigible."

"I don't like you going off with strangers," he said, gently rather than critically. "Especially late at night."

"Simon isn't a stranger," she replied dreamily. "I feel as if I'd known him all my life. And if you really don't trust him, I can tell you that I gave him all sorts of chances to kidnap me . . . hoping he would . . . but he didn't."

Hyram Angelworth smiled and shook his head. "I'm afraid you're the one who's incorrigible."

She became aware that Richard Hamlin had materialised near the entrance to the adjacent study off the main room. He was ostensibly looking through some papers, but listening as always. Didn't he ever sleep? And didn't it ever occur to him that she might like to talk to her father alone?

She tossed her handbag on to a sofa and kicked off her shoes, trying not to let her irritation get the better of her.

"We did have a sort of adventure, though." She flopped into a chair and pointed her toes and stretched her legs. "In my efforts to get myself kidnapped I lured Simon into a sleazy bar—Sammy's Booze & Billiards, to be precise."

An expression of intense pain developed on her father's face as she recited the full name of Sammy's establishment, which only served to encourage her to continue with greater relish.

"Simon wasn't keen to go in, but I insisted, and there were these very underworld-looking characters playing pool, and Simon recognised one of them and called him by name. He didn't remember until too late that this guy named Brad Ryner was a detective, and so he was probably pretending to be a crook to collect information for the police. Ryner claimed his name was Joe and he'd never seen Simon before. He really acted nasty.

Simon's worried to death he may have gotten this detective in trouble. Isn't that thrilling?"

"It's troubling," Angelworth growled. "It's bad enough to know there are so many crooks and parasites in the world without having to worry that my own daughter's out rubbing elbows with them. I can't say I think much of your friend for taking you to a place like that."

"I needled him into it. I've been there a couple of times before, with the gang, and I wanted to see how he'd take it."

"And what about this man Templar? We don't know a thing about him. Why should he recognise a plainclothes policeman?"

Carole stood up, suddenly wanting to end the conversation as soon as she could.

"Well, at least he recognised the policeman instead of the crooks—if they were crooks." She touched him on the shoulder. "It's all over anyway, Daddy. I'm really tired, and you must be too. Good night."

He was still brooding in his chair as she went down the hall to her bedroom, and she wondered if Richard Hamlin would be commenting on her escapade after she had left.

CHAPTER 3

Two alternatives duelled in Simon Templar's mind: One claimed that the best thing he could do for Brad Ryner was to stay as far away from him as possible, hoping that Ryner's playmates would forget the whole episode if they were not reminded of it; the other rebutted that having inadvertently placed Ryner in danger, the Saint owed it to him to get back in touch with him and help him in any way possible.

When logic was deadlocked, the Saint was inclined to let his instincts take over. He literally found himself driving towards Sammy's Booze & Billiards before his rational mind had reached a conclusion.

Simon made no effort to resist the decision of his reflexes. His mind went on to process future possibilities. If Ryner was still at the pool table with his companions then the Saint would ignore them and try to follow Ryner when he left the bar. If the three men had left, he would try to trace one or more of them.

He had faultlessly memorised the route, in reverse, on the way back to the New Sylvania, and retracing it this time was no problem.

The neighbourhood of Sammy's bar was a hodgepodge of shabby and squalid in the creeping process of becoming one hundred per cent squalid. Sammy's was at the approximate half-way point of decay, and the Saint had to slow down sharply in order to avoid a couple of unsteady drunks who staggered into the road just ahead of him as he came within a block of the bar.

It occurred to him later that if those two alcohol-laden human tankers had not pitched and rolled across his path at just that time, Brad Ryner might have died. Because it was when Simon jammed on the brakes that the edge of his field of vision picked up a trace of movement in an alley to his right. It might have been a cat. It might have been some nocturnal stroller taking a short cut home. It might have been a newspaper blown by the wind that was whipping a few drops of rain against the windows of his car.

But the Saint was so keyed up and watchful that he could not ignore even such an undefined flash of motion in a dark place near Sammy's bar. He pulled immediately over to the kerb under a no-parking sign about fifty feet beyond. He was out of the car in an instant, sprinting back along the sidewalk to the mouth of the alley. There he stopped short, drizzle sprinkling his face and wilting his clothes, and listened. There was an ominous economy in what he heard: feet scuffing on pavement, muffled thumps, a sudden stifled expulsion of cries . . .

The Saint judged the distance of the sounds down the alley, then catapulted into action. He knew that surprise would favour him for only a few seconds, but those few seconds were all he needed. His long legs carried him down the alley so fast that he just had time to take in the rudiments of the shadowy scene before he made physical contact with it: one man holding another while a third punched and kicked him.

The big man who was doing the beating turned with fist raised as the Saint bore down on him like some wild spectre set free by the night wind. The man's flabbergasted defense would have had some effect against a less swift and co-ordinated blitzkrieg than the Saint's, because this was the very big brawny man from the pool room, towering in the semidarkness with a trace of street-light touching the raindrops on his sallow face, sparking a glint of squinting eyes and clenched teeth.

In spite of his size, he was caught off balance and the Saint hit him with approximately the effect of a locomotive striking a straw scarecrow. The man who had been a moment before slamming knuckles and shoe-leather into his defenseless victim did not exactly fly apart in several pieces, but he did the next thing to it. He was smashed back against the brick wall of the building forming one side of the alley, and fell away from it with the limp awkward grace of a dropped rag doll.

Simon Templar did not believe that his charge had done more than temporarily decommission the night football player, but he had to turn and meet a new problem. There was a glint of bright metal to his right, where the victim of the beating lay on the pavement. The man who had been holding him was a fat seal-like shape spearheaded with the long blade of a knife. The Saint was poised to receive an attack, but it did not come. The stout man slid through the shadows like a bloated fish through murky waters, always keeping the knife-point straight at the Saint. It became clear that he was more enthusiastic about getting away to the far end of the alley, away from the brightly lit street where Simon's car was parked, than he was about giving battle.

Simon stalked him, as the fat man backed steadily away from the scene of combat. When the Saint increased his own pace, the other, never turning, quickened his, moving with surprising agility for a man so rotund. Still, Simon would have caught him, or run him down like a lion after a water buffalo, if there had not been a sudden scuff of steps behind the Saint's back. Before he could turn, an arm locked round his throat like a thick noose. In the same instant, though, while his attacker was still in motion, Simon ducked forward and spun to the side, smashing the man behind him into the wall with an elbow driven back deep into his belly.

The Saint's instant reactions weakened the big man's hold enough to allow Simon to slip his head free. Meanwhile his stout comrade seemed to be encumbered by no inner conflicts about teamwork or loyalty. He took off for the other end of the alley without ever looking back. The other, taking advantage of the fact that the Saint had dropped to one knee in escaping the arm-lock on his neck, and having literally lost stomach for continuing the battle on his own, likewise turned and stumbled down the alley in pursuit of his portly pal.

Simon decided that Brad Ryner's condition was more crucial than chasing down the men who had been beating him. He had a sickening feeling that he might already have been too late to save the policeman. The punishment he had been taking when the Saint arrived at the alley had looked more like a sadistic way of finishing him off permanently than just a rough lesson in the wages of spying.

The detective seemed lifeless when the Saint knelt beside him; his face and clothing were sticky with blood. But Simon could detect breath and a pulse-beat. He would have preferred not to move the man alone, risking worse damage, but he could not leave him there while he went for help. He picked him up in his arms as gently as he could and carried him to the street.

As he came out of the alley onto the sidewalk, stepping slowly and heavily under the weight of his burden, he saw a sight that even under the circumstances struck him as almost comically ironic: Parked in front of his own car in the no-parking zone was a police patrol car, and a uniformed officer was standing in the rain, busily writing out a ticket.

100

Another patrolman, less engrossed, spotted Simon first, jumped out of the police car, and strode towards him.

"Whaddaya think you're doing?" he interrogated brilliantly.

Simon, still trudging forward with his bloodstained load, told him: "Carrying coals to Newcastle, maybe. Your department probably knows about this chap. He's an under-cover agent from California named Brad Ryner. He was getting beaten up in that alley when I came along."

The policeman looked at the crimson mess that had been Ryner's face.

"God damn!" he breathed.

"I'm afraid you wouldn't recognise him right now even if you knew him," Simon said.

"Who are you?" the other patrolman asked.

"The good Samaritan. Don't you think we'd better get this man to a hospital before we fill out a report in triplicate?"

The first policeman helped Simon deposit Ryner in the patrol car. The second pointed: "Is that your car?"

"I confess," Simon replied. "When I saw somebody getting killed in that alley I didn't take time to hunt up a parking lot."

The officer ripped up the ticket he had been writing and dropped the fragments in the gutter, under a lamp-post sign warning about the penalties for depositing litter.

"What did you say his name is?"

"Ryner." Simon spelled it. "Brad Ryner. I knew him slightly on the Coast, and I spotted him in Sammy's boozer more than an hour ago."

"You better come along with us," the patrolman said, which was no more and no less than the Saint could have expected.

A moment later, siren howling, they were racing through the rain-swept streets.

It was eleven o'clock in the morning before Brad Ryner was able to talk to him. Even before Ryner had regained consciousness, just after daybreak, a tired but conscientious detective lieutenant had been called from his bed to oversee developments at the hospital, while a uniformed guard had been assigned to the door of Ryner's room. Simon, meanwhile, after being thoroughly identified, had returned to his hotel at about four in the morning, on his own condition that he be phoned as soon as Ryner could talk. The call came at 10:15, and he was at the hospital twenty minutes later.

Brad Ryner was propped up in his bed, half sitting, one eye and half his face covered with bandages, when Simon entered the room.

"I almost hope you don't remember me," said the Saint grimly. "I wish I hadn't remembered you. Calling your name was the stupidest thing I've done for a hundred years."

The exposed half of Ryner's face was heavily bruised; even so, the corner of his broad mouth managed a trace of a smile.

"Just the breaks of the game," he said in a voice that sounded as if it came through a wad of cotton. "Don't blame yourself, Simon."

"I won't waste time blaming myself. I'd rather know what I can do to make up for it."

"You already made up for it," Ryner said indistinctly. "You saved my life. Another minute or two and those bastards would have killed me."

"That's like thanking a man who's stabbed you for pulling the knife out," Simon said ruefully.

"You're exaggerating," said a new voice, and a tall, slender, prematurely grey-haired man who had been standing by the side of the bed stepped forward to shake Simon's hand. "I'm Stacey, detective lieutenant. I was responsible for getting Brad here for this job in the first place."

From there Lieutenant Stacey went on to say how pleased and intrigued he was to meet the famous Saint.

"Apparently nobody's identity is safe round here," Simon responded. "But now that you've seen an example of my genius in action you'll understand how I got to be so notorious. The only excuse I can think of for blabbing Brad's name is that I was under the spell of a beautiful young lady at the time."

"You're not kidding," said Ryner.

"But just mentioning his name shouldn't have blown the whole thing," Lieutenant Stacey said. "Those hoods couldn't know that somebody named Brad Ryner was a police officer out in California, and you didn't press the point, did you?"

Simon shook his head.

"I hopped away like a flea off a hot griddle."

"So why didn't they just accept it as a case of mistaken identity? You don't go out and kill one of your pool buddies just because some stranger thinks he's somebody he used to know by another name."

"They might have been suspicious already," Simon suggested.

"I don't know," Brad Ryner said. "I didn't realise it if they were, but of course they wouldn't have told me if they smelled a rat, since I was the rat."

"There's no point wasting time theorising about that," Stacey said. "What's done is done. It's a rotten shame, though, even if it was nobody's fault."

"Yeah," said Ryner, shifting painfully in his bed. "I'm on the sidelines permanently as far as this game is concerned, and there's nobody else on our side playing."

"You mean playing under-cover?" Simon asked.

"Right," Ryner croaked. "The lieutenant here already had one New York man disappear on this job; that's why he called me in."

"Sounds tough," Simon said with growing interest. "What's the game exactly?"

Lieutenant Stacey looked questioningly at Ryner. Ryner attempted a nod of approval.

"Have a chair," Stacey said to the Saint, and the two men sat down beside the bed.

"It's tough all right," Stacey said. "We're on the trail of a guy who's getting all the organised crime in these parts sewn up.

He makes the Mafia look like the Dead End Kids. When he gets finished, the only thing he won't run in this state will be the clocks."

"I suppose it would be superfluous to ask why you don't arrest him," Simon said. "No hard evidence?"

"Not only that," Lieutenant Stacey said with a helpless gesture, "we don't even know who he is."

"That does make it difficult."

"Evidence?" Ryner put in weakly. "There's evidence all over the place, but it never leads to the top."

"We've made arrests," Stacey said. "Even got a few convictions—which isn't easy, considering this guy seems to have half the judges in his pocket, and the witnesses have a way of vanishing or forgetting everything but their own names. But even the thugs who carry out his orders don't know who the boss is. They call him the Supremo. We've found out that much."

"Big deal," Ryner said. "They could call him Sitting Bull, for all the good it does us."

"And we know a few other fairly useless facts," Stacey went on. "Such as the fact that some of the Supremo's muscle men hang out at Sammy's Booze & Billiards."

"Is Sammy's some kind of a headquarters or communications centre?" Simon asked.

"No," Ryner answered. "Strictly for amusement."

"But there is a club we think may be an operations centre for the organisation . . ." Stacey hesitated. "Why should I be taking up your time with all this? I'm sure you've got plenty to do on your visit here without listening to a cop's tales of woe."

Simon smiled.

"What you mean is, why should you be divulging information to somebody who's not on your team?"

"Maybe," the lieutenant conceded, "although Brad's told me you can be trusted come hell or high water, and I know enough about you to realise that you're your own man. You'd never work for the Supremo or any other gang boss."

"I appreciate the confidence," Simon said to Brad Ryner. "I wish I'd lived up to it better last night. Now I suspect you're back to square one."

"We never got past square one," Ryner assured him. "The most I ever found out was some information about some little frogs in a mighty big pond."

"And now we won't even be getting that much," Lieutenant Stacey said morosely. "We're right where we were six months ago, and I'd be willing to bet we'll be in exactly the same place a year from now."

Simon stood up suddenly and paced across the white antiseptic room.

"Not necessarily," he said.

Ryner, who had closed his one visible eye, opened it again. Stacey turned in his chair to peer up into the Saint's intent face.

"You know something us public servants don't know?"

"No," Simon answered. "But if you'll let me, I might be able to help you."

CHAPTER 4

It was a strange offer for the Saint to make, and an uncharacteristic way for him to word it: *But if you'll let me, I might be able to help you.* Stacey had been right; Simon Templar did not work for big or little Caesars. He did not work for anybody but himself. Yet in the circumstances his usual motives were thrust into the background, temporarily at least, because of the responsibility he felt for what had happened to Brad Ryner in trying to expose the man known as the Supremo.

"Look," he said to the two detectives. "Brad was brought into this game because he wasn't known in Philadelphia. I got him knocked out of the game, right on his head, even if I didn't know what I was doing. What you do when that happens in football is send in a substitute. Well, here I am."

The silence that followed was full of astonishment, doubt, and awe of the net of red tape that was bound to descend upon anyone who departed from officially marked paths of police investigation.

"You ain't thinking of becoming a cop, are you?" Brad Ryner asked nervously.

"I was thinking more in terms of becoming a fellow-traveller."

"Before I say anything," Stacey said cautiously, "I'd better find out exactly what you have in mind."

"I have an idea for getting close to the Supremo," Simon said. "Possibly even face to face with him. And I'm in a good position to do it: I'm from out of town—further out than Brad was. I have a breath-taking gift for bamboozling people. I have a fantastic record of successfully overwhelming criminals of every size and shape. And I have the strength of ten because my heart is pure."

"Bravo," Ryner said feebly. "Bravo!"

Lieutenant Stacey looked fascinated but dubious.

"It's very good of you to think of doing something like that, but I'm not even sure I could consider . . . Even if I felt convinced it was the best thing, I don't have the authority to . . ."

"Would it help any if I told you I intend to go ahead and do it anyway, no matter what you decide?" The Saint's expression was not so much defiant as blandly innocent, as if he were making an announcement of what he intended to have for his lunch.

Lieutenant Stacey came out with a kind of snorting laugh, because it was all he could think of to come out with. Ryner was too uncomfortable to waste his breath.

"Good," he said with conviction. "You do it. But what is it?"

"What's the name of that club you mentioned, that the Supremo's gang uses as an operational HQ?"

"The Pear Tree," Lieutenant Stacey replied. "Do you know of it?"

"Only by name," the Saint answered. "Very elegant spot, I've heard."

"This is a very elegant crew," Stacey said.

"I could tell that last night," Simon remarked. "That large gentleman had a very refined way of putting his dancing pumps into Brad's stomach."

"Those were just the floor-sweepings of the gang," Brad Ryner said. "I had to start somewhere."

"Well, I intend to start at The Pear Tree," Simon told them. "My first job is going to be to get somebody other than the bouncer or the headwaiter to listen to me. I may have to use a little muscle, but somehow or other I'll get word up the communications lines that I have to see the big chief."

"Big chief, big deal!" Ryner said sceptically. "I might as well walk into the White House and say I have to see the President."

"But if you were the ambassador from France, you wouldn't have much trouble getting an appointment."

"So where are you an ambassador from?"

"West Coast Kelly."

The name West Coast Kelly did not, at that time, require further explanation. To the California-Nevada kingdom of high crimes and misdemeanors, West Coast Kelly was as Stalin to Russia or Perón to Argentina. Once a lover of publicity, fond of grinning newspaper photographs of his moustachioed self arm-in-arm with rapturous movie starlets, he had been taught, by a couple of all-expense-paid vacations in Alcatraz and three generous but noisy attempts to send him into peaceful retirement at Elysian Fields Cemetery, the value of privacy and seclusion. He still ran the rackets, still commanded felonious armies, still manipulated vast wealth, but had become almost as aloof as Philadelphia's Supremo. He did his business through subalterns; and it had been rumoured recently that he was yearning for new worlds to conquer, sending out feelers to areas beyond his long conceded territory. So there was nothing too fantastic in the Saint's suggestion that he might pose as one of West Coast Kelly's emissaries. Brad Ryner and Lieutenant Stacey acknowledged that much without question.

"But what news does the ambassador bring?" Stacey enquired.

107

"That West Coast Kelly has big plans of his own for Philly. To put it bluntly, Kelly wants a big slice of the pie here, or he threatens to take over the whole show."

"Not very subtle, but it might get the Supremo to listen," Stacey granted. "You might even arrange it so Kelly's instructed you not to speak to anybody but the top man himself."

"Easy enough," Simon said, "since I'm giving my own orders."

"Easy!" Ryner snorted. "You'll see how easy it is to get your head blown off. Don't you think they'll check out on the West Coast to see if you're for real?"

"Whom do they check with? They'd have to get on to Kelly himself to prove that his personal ambassador wasn't really sent by him." Simon was moving restlessly round the room. "Anyway, my idea isn't to become a permanent fixture round the place. All I want to do is barge straight in and see how close I can get to the Supreme Stinko. I think he could feel so threatened that he'll at least have to listen."

Stacey rubbed his chin.

"But what happens then? The Supremo's still going to keep his identity a secret, or do something to cover up his tracks."

Simon came to a halt again beside the bed.

"I'll just have to play it by ear from there," he said. "You don't try to predict a chess match before you've seen the opening."

"I dunno," Ryner finally admitted. "I guess any plan is better than none. And if you've stayed alive this long, you might stay alive through this, but I doubt it."

"With those cheering words, off I go into the fray."

Stacey stood up.

"What can I say? There's nothing I want worse than the Supremo. Or even just to know his initials, or where he gets his hair cut, or what shaving lotion he uses. But how can I author-ise . . ."

"You don't need to," said the Saint. "Just give me a telephone number where I can reach you. I'm going to visit The Pear Tree tonight and see what kind of partridges are roosting in it."

Only after he got back to the New Sylvania after lunch did he remember that he had promised Carole Angelworth that he would phone her. He had no lack of reminders: According to notes in his box, she had already called him three times.

He settled down in an armchair in his room, had the switchboard dial her number, and after one ring heard her voice saying breathlessly: "Hullo?"

"Hullo. This is Simon. How are things?"

"Oh, I was so worried about you! I thought you'd be calling me earlier, and when I tried getting you a couple of hours ago and you weren't there, and nobody knew where you were, I was sure you'd gotten yourself killed."

"I thought you'd be catching up on your beauty sleep and I didn't want to disturb it, so I went out and made a sort of duty call on a sick friend."

"I'm sorry, but it's already half-past two, and I was hoping I could show you round a little today. I hope you haven't gone and made other plans."

One thing that Simon had decided was not to give Carole even a hint of what he was up to in connection with the Supremo. The way she was behaving now satisfied him that he had been right: Even if he could have trusted her completely not to babble to anyone, she would have driven him crazy with hysterical concern for his safety.

"I do have some business to attend to this evening," he confessed.

"This *evening?* Why in the world do you have to work at night?"

"I carry on all kinds of mysterious activities at all sorts of strange hours. It's one of the things about me that makes me so fatally attractive to innocent young girls."

Her pout was audible.

"This afternoon then? You won't be in town for ever. Can't you spare a couple of hours?"

Simon could have used a couple of hours' rest, having had

very little the night before, and anticipating very little for the night to come, but he found himself saying: "All right; I'll meet you in half an hour."

"Wonderful!" Carole bubbled. "Half an hour. In the garage—this time we'll take my car."

When he had hung up, Simon wondered why he had surrendered so easily. He discovered, in scanning his feelings, that it was not only that he did not want to disappoint her, but also—a little disconcertingly—that he would have been disappointed if he had not seen her.

CHAPTER 5

At seven o'clock, Simon and Carole were in a midtown cocktail lounge whose soft leather, velvet draperies, and impressionistic nudes were in considerable contrast to the hospitality of Sammy's Booze & Billiards. A "couple of hours" had stretched quite painlessly into four.

"I have to admit," Simon remarked, "that this is the first time I've ever had a whirlwind tour of an orphanage, a clinic for retarded children, and the offices of a vigilance committee, all in the same day.

Carole sat closer to him that even the limits of their banquette required, sipping a frozen Daiquiri.

"I suppose it's not what you'd call light entertainment," she said. "Were you bored?"

"No. Your father's good works are very impressive, and you could make a visit to Independence Hall seem like more fun than a trip to the Folies Bergères."

"I'm glad I could show you round instead of Dick Hamlin. I bet he'd have taken over, the next time he met you."

"How does he get on with the Law Enforcement watchdogs?"

"Why, he's their prize exhibit . . . Let's forget him!"

She slipped her arm round his. Throughout the afternoon, Simon had become more and more conscious that the effervescent, happily chattering girl beside him was much more emotionally involved with him than would have seemed possible in such a short time.

The Saint was accustomed to the admiration of women. Nature had endowed him with that almost unbelievably handsome face which, combined with his other attributes of mind and body, made him as irresistible to the female sex as a fox to a pack of hounds. But in this case he was dealing with a very susceptible girl who was obviously looking for something much more serious than a few days of fun. As much as Simon was also attracted to her, and tempting as it was to give free rein to his hormones, he felt an obligation to avoid doing or saying anything that would draw her more deeply into the pit of disappointment she was digging for herself.

Now she was snuggling against him, and when he glanced at her, her eyes had that same poignant, misty, searching look that had disturbed him more than once during the afternoon. It was as if the real Carole, vulnerable and love-seeking, was for just a moment breaking through the razzle-dazzle of words and laughs that normally fluttered gaily between her and the rest of the world.

"Couldn't you cancel that miserable business deal you *say* you've got lined up for tonight," she pleaded, "and we can do something a little more exciting than look at orphans? I feel I owe it to you. After all, I'm the one who dragged you through Daddy's charities. It probably shows a lack of self-confidence. Trying to build myself up vicariously by trotting out the good works of the paterfamilias. If I thought I could really trust myself to interest you, all on my own, I'd probably have taken you for a walk in the country."

"Are you sure you didn't major in psychology instead of sociology?" Simon bantered.

"A fortuneteller told me I need to live less in my head and more in my heart."

Simon looked down into his glass noncommittally.

111

"I won't try to compete with your fortuneteller, but I can tell you one thing: You don't need Daddy or anybody else to make you interesting."

"Give me a chance to prove it then," she said eagerly, not letting go his arm.

"How?"

"Well, unless you're really going out with another woman tonight, couldn't you finish up your business early enough for us to get together? I could show you my prize-winning college essays or something, just to prove I'm a great kid all on my own."

"You've already proved it," Simon assured her. He was thinking fast. Should he break with her right now, knowing he would have to leave her behind before many days had passed anyway? Or should he let her down gently, striking a delicate balance between encouraging her too much and hurting her unnecessarily? The second choice seemed best. "Wouldn't it be better to wait till tomorrow, though? I'm not sure what time I'll get through tonight."

She moved away from him a little, took a swallow of her drink, and looked at him with sly eyes over the rim of the glass.

"*Are* you going out with another woman?"

"Incredible as it may seem, I've managed to evade my panting pursuers, and the most exciting thing I can look forward to is a bottle of good wine with dinner."

"Then you'll see me after dinner? I mean, if you want to. If you don't want to, don't bother." She suddenly broke her mock seriousness and laughed. "I really sound like a fool, don't I? All these games I'm playing with you. But I'd really like it if you wanted to do something later this evening."

Simon looked at his watch.

"If I start out soon, I just might finish before good little girls are all tucked up in bed."

"I'll wait up. I can afford to miss some sleep on the off-chance that I'll get some relief from the stupefying social life I've been leading."

They left the bar, stepped out into the perfume of exhaust fumes and the multicoloured city substitutes for moonlight, and walked to where she had parked her Lincoln convertible. Somehow, even with the best intentions, he had managed to more or less commit himself to Carole on that evening when he was already scheduled to risk his neck in a venture that could take an unpredictable number of hours. Apparently the current of their relationship flowed both ways to a greater extent than he wanted to admit to himself. Or was it a desire to unravel the girl's feelings and set everything straight and clear before the tides of his life carried him away from her again?

Whatever the reason, he was assuming that he was going to complete his expedition to the Supremo's presumed operations centre in time to see Carole again that night. He did not have optimistic visions of himself knocking on a door, saying his piece about West Coast Kelly, and being ushered with feverish haste into the throne room of the Supremo himself. He hoped instead to make contact with appropriate underlings, announce his supposed identity and mission, then leave the night club and wait for some action the next day.

He opened the car door for Carole, but made no move to get in beside her.

"Can't I drop you off, wherever you're going?" she offered. "Or are you afraid I'll attack the other woman?"

"I'm afraid of her attacking you," he replied, in exactly the same mischievous tone. "You're not quite unknown in this town. A cab will be more discreet."

"I'll see you later, then."

"It's hard for me to make a promise, but if anything holds me up later than ten-thirty or eleven I'll give you a ring."

The Pear Tree was one of those places whose portals are virtually indistinguishable from their residential neighbours except

113

upon close inspection. Along a quiet street of dignified apartments, its unobtrusive heavy wooden door betrayed its commercial genus only by a pair of long Spanish tile panels flanking it, whose glazed colours illustrated the arboreal namesake of the place. A more inquisitive search would then have discovered the small brass plaque on the door itself, engraved in copybook script with the words *The Pear Tree.*

Simon opened the door and found himself immediately confronted by a very large man in a tuxedo that looked as if it might have been forged from the same material used to make old black iron stoves. At least it gave an impression of such stiffness and weightiness, and was so vast and cylindrical around the man's torso, that the comparison with a huge pot-bellied stove was irresistible. Perhaps the first thing the Saint definitely deduced about his faceless quarry was that the Supremo had a taste for over-sized myrmidons.

"Good evening, sir," the iron cask rumbled. "How many, please?"

"Just one."

"For dinner?"

"Yes."

"Very good."

Simon was passed on to a beautifully dressed platinum blonde who in various ways might have symbolised a pear-bearing tree whose fruits were just passing the maximum of ripeness. There would be nothing too brash, too hurried here. From the dim red recesses of the bar where she guided him came a delicate ripple of piano music. A starched and freshly shaved headwaiter took his order while he savoured a dry martini on the rocks.

The dining room had the same restrained, polished plushness of the rest of the establishment. It was not easy to imagine that this compartment of elegance in the midst of middle-aged Main-Lineage could be the epicentre of a criminal empire, but the Saint had long since stopped feeling surprise at the discrepancies between appearance and reality, between façade and inner fact.

As he ate his lobster thermidor, he watched for any sign that this particular room, with its damask-covered tables and silver ice buckets, its fresh flowers and candles in tinted crystal, might be hosting something more sinister than well-heeled and well-served dinner guests. True, a few of the male diners possessed shoulders and features that looked more as if they had been formed in the saloons and gyms of New York's Lower East Side than on the playing fields of Princeton, but that in itself proved nothing except the levelling potential of worldly success.

Only one feature of the room engaged the Saint's attention more than any other, and that was a door at the rear marked PRIVATE. Such a door was not particularly unusual. In fact the world was full of doors marked private that concealed nothing more mysterious than adding machines, toilets, or supplies of clean towels. But this door, which never opened while the Saint was eating his meal, was at least a promising starting point for exploration.

Now a man less blessed with courage and a flair for dramatic direct action than Simon Templar was might have made discreet enquiries about the nature of the room labelled private, might have requested an audience with the manager, or might have done any number of things less effective than what he did.

He finished his lobster, swallowed the last of his Bollinger, got up from his table, and walked over to the door marked private.

He had scarcely applied his knuckles to the varnished wood when his waiter, a nervous little man whose head-hair was entirely concentrated in a miniature black mop under his nose, raced up to him and tapped him on the arm.

"Don't put your hands on me, Bug-face," the Saint ordered him coarsely, "or I'll play 'Turkey in the Straw' with my heels all up and down your backbone."

Suddenly a red-hot skillet could not have seemed less attractive to the waiter's touch than the Saint's forearm. Simon's natural inflections had been flattened out for the occasion into a raspy Western accent, and his face had a cruel toughness that would have made a chunk of flint seem mushy by comparison.

"Was something wrong with your dinner, sir?" the waiter asked with quavering unctuousness.

"Where's the manager?" Simon barked back.

The waiter was making frantic gestures in the air with one hand while trying to keep the Saint appeased with a servile smile.

"If you'll tell me what was wrong . . ."

Simon bent over him menacingly.

"Look, you pinheaded spaghetti-wrangler, I won't talk to anybody but the manager."

The suave headwaiter arrived on the scene, more self-possessed than his colleague.

"What seems to be the trouble, sir?" he enquired smoothly.

"What the hell use are you?" Simon growled. "Are you going to knock this door down for me? What do I have to do to see the manager here—dynamite the joint?"

He reckoned that the more noise he made, the sooner he would be admitted to the inner sanctum. With one possible danger: a bouncer (Simon had already spotted the black barrel shape of the front-door greeter taking an interest from the dining-room entrance) might simply try to throw him out. The Saint was confident that he could throw the bouncer out instead, but he preferred a less devious way of getting the attention of the higher ups. He banged harder on the private door.

The headwaiter, who was no more a roughhouse type than his subordinate, glanced around to locate the tuxedoed gorilla, who moved unobtrusively down one side of the dining room towards them.

"If you would please tell me what your complaint is," the headwaiter said placatingly, "I'll be glad to—"

"I don't have no complaint," Simon said. "I'm here on business, and I wanna see the manager."

He continued pounding on the door. Just before the bouncer reached him, the barrier swung partially open. A surly crinkly-haired head appeared, and a voice said, "What's going on out here?"

The Saint sensed the bouncer behind him, about to grasp his arms if necessary, and he decided that the moment for crossing this particular Rubicon had come. With a strength given added force by swiftness and surprise, he shoved the door farther open, stepped inside the private room, slammed the door again and turned the metal knob that threw the bolt. He did it so quickly that the three men behind him were left standing flat-footed in the dining room, excluded entirely from even the sound of the ensuing proceedings.

In front of Simon was the temporarily flustered man who had opened the door. Three other men sat on sofas or chairs, while another came to his feet behind a desk at the rear of the room. Within two seconds, two pistols had appeared.

Simon carefully showed the nature of his intentions by keeping his hands away from his body.

"Sorry to bust in like this," he murmured, "but I've got important business that can't wait." Then he verbally lit the fuse of his private brand of dynamite and tossed it hissing into the centre of the room. "I want to see the Supremo."

CHAPTER 6

A naked belly dancer erupting from a nine-layer cake at a conclave of the College of Cardinals could not have produced more of a sensation than Simon Templar did when he presented himself in the private room of the club Pear Tree. The hefty characters who had been decorating the furniture were all at attention, but their vocal cords were temporarily out of contact with their brains.

Although the Saint was now looking down the steel throats of four pistols, he relaxed. The character he was portraying never smiled, as Simon himself might have done under similar circumstances. Instead he swept his gaze from one side of the room to

117

the other, taking in everyone and everything, while his lips held an arrogant sneer.

It was a very expensively furnished room, but designed for business, not for guests. There were as many telephones as there were pistols. There were two radios, two television sets, several filing cabinets, and a stock ticker, along with other knobbed and dialed devices which the Saint did not have time to identify. His new friends obviously liked to keep up with what was going on in the world. The place, on the face of it, looked more like a communications centre than a restaurant manager's office, and that was exactly what Simon had expected.

The man behind the desk finally got his tongue back in touch with his cerebrum.

"Who the hell are you?" he snapped.

A couple of the men in the room, the two who had been fastest with their pistols, looked fairly brutish. This one had blond hair and an Ivy League accent. His blue silk tie was enviable; in more normal times, the Saint would have cheerfully complimented him on it.

"You're not the Supremo," Simon said roughly.

"I know what I'm not," the other answered. He realised that he was clutching the edge of his desk, and eased his hands away. "I asked you who you are."

"I'm somebody who wants to see the Supremo."

The blond man jerked a half smile at one of his colleagues.

"What's a Supremo—a cigar? You'll find them in the lobby. By God, I'm going to have Ansel's ears for letting drunks wander all over this building." He focussed cold turquoise eyes on the Saint again. "This is a business meeting, and you've got n business here."

"Funny," Simon remarked, "it looks more like a shooting gallery. Or what are you scared of?"

The man at the desk drew back his shoulders.

"I'm not going to explain our security measures to you. I suggest you walk out of here right now, or else take your choice of being thrown out on your head or being arrested."

"I've come too far to walk out," Simon said flatly. "You say this is a business meeting. Well, I got business. But it's got to be with the Supremo or nobody."

"I'd put my money on nobody," one of the other men said. "Are you walking out or getting carried out?"

"I guess you guys have heard of West Coast Kelly," Simon said. "That's who I'm talking for."

He was expecting the announcement to have an interesting impact, and his disappointment was catastrophic. For at the same moment as it should have been registering, a door at the back of the room opened, and in walked the fat seal-like man Simon had met the night before.

He blinked exactly three times as his mouth formed a large O and his dewlaps dropped to his collarbones.

"That's him!" he squealed. "That's him—the sonovabitch I told you about, from Sammy's!"

It was one of those disastrous sneaky backhanders with which a malicious Fate delights in upsetting applecarts, which a pessimist might have predicted but an optimist had no way to guard against. The Saint tried his best to cope with it, but even his inventiveness had been caught flat-footed.

"Sure, I stopped you and your meat-head pal from killing a cop who'd been playing you for suckers. I figured it was worth more to sell myself to him as a good guy, and get an 'in' that we could all use."

"You didn't need to play-act as hard as that!"

The seal, mindful of the juggernaut that had smitten him and his comrade in the rain-swept alley, was not about to calm down. He kept shouting, machine-gunning blasts of accusation round the room, urging the others to do something. As on the previous night, he did not place himself physically in the forefront of the battle, but the situation was still going his way.

119

Simon took a step back towards the door.

"Maybe I'd better drop round later, when you've all calmed down," he said diplomatically.

"Don't let him get out!" the seal howled.

The man behind the desk confirmed the order, and four thugs reached the Saint at the same instant. Simon's hands, elbows, knees, and feet became deadly weapons. One of his attackers dropped to the floor, squirming in agony. A second staggered back, half blinded by a blow to his face that sent a cascade of blood streaming down over his lips and chin. But a fist caught Simon hard on his own jaw, slamming him back against the wall. Two apes were on him like one four-armed monster, and a knee in his stomach knocked the wind momentarily out of him. The seal was hopping up and down, trying to see the centre of the melee. Simon braced himself against the wall and managed to ram the toe of his right shoe into the solar plexus of one of his attackers, sending the man backwards into the seal. The two of them bounced across the carpet like bowling pins.

It was a satisfying sight, but the last that Simon saw for several hours. He was bashed on the head with something very hard. The room seemed to fill with black water, which rose very rapidly from floor to ceiling. The shouts and grunts and heavy breaths faded to silence.

There was no more of anything until after a timeless time he became strangely and vaguely aware of his own existence. He seemed to be floating in nowhere, unable to see or hear. His mind was not functioning at a level that would allow him even to wonder who or where he was. His being was a small unstable ball of pain. He felt his arm being manipulated, and a momentary new pinpoint of pain, and then nothingness again.

Carole Angelworth waited for his promised call until eleven-thirty. Her phone rang twice during the evening, but neither of those calls was the one she wanted.

She couldn't really believe that he would stand her up deliberately. It wouldn't be like him to lie. He would just have told her when he had left her at the end of the afternoon that he couldn't possibly make it that night.

She was full of self-doubts. Had she thrown herself at him so obviously that he wanted to hurt her in order to get rid of her? Had she bored him to death with that tour of her father's charities?

She wasn't used to being refused anything that she wanted—a dress, a trinket, a car, or a man. She knew she was spoiled, but that didn't make it any easier to swallow a rejection. She had decided that she was madly in love. And now the man she was in love with was half an hour late phoning her. And the worst of it was that she felt a strange foreboding, an apprehension that could not be explained by the logical part of her mind.

She picked up the hotel phone and asked for his room. It didn't answer.

She felt a need to talk to her father again, as she had always done when faced with anything beyond her ordinary capacity to handle. She went down the hall and through the living-room and found him in his study.

Richard Hamlin was there too, inevitably, carrying on an earnest conversation at her father's big desk. He stopped speaking immediately and stood up, greeting her with the toothy, slightly deferential grin that he apparently thought would someday win her trust, if not her affection. He preferred hanging about in the background, almost shyly, where he could pretend not to notice what was going on, and where he could at least hope that no one was noticing him. But whenever confronted directly he came up with that same grin, which Carole had once said reminded her of a slightly dishonest medieval sheepherder tugging his forelock at his feudal lord's daughter.

"Well, ready for bed?" her father asked, leaning back in his chair.

"Not really," Carole answered. She walked up to the desk and said quite rudely: "Richard, I wish you weren't here every time

I come in. But just this once, I'd like to speak to my father alone."

Hamlin looked at Hyram Angelworth, who nodded. Carole waited until her father's man Friday had left the study and then got straight to the point. She felt secure in this room, with its warm pine panelling, heavy leather upholstering, and massive, solid furniture.

"I'm very worried about Simon," she began, "and don't tell me you don't know who Simon is."

Her father had a habit of ignoring the existence of male friends of hers whom he did not approve of.

"It would be a little hard for me not to have heard the name," he said indulgently. "You've mentioned it at least thirty times in the past twenty-four hours. Exactly what is it you're worried about?"

"He had some business tonight, and I made him promise to call me by eleven, and he hasn't done it."

The springs of Hyram Angelworth's desk chair squeaked lightly as he leaned further back and shrugged.

"Catastrophe," he sympathised. "I can remember occasionally being kept busy after eleven at night myself. Why don't you just stop fretting and get some sleep? I don't doubt that you'll track him down in the morning."

Carole settled on the edge of the desk and looked seriously at him.

"This isn't something to joke about," she said. "I'm in love with him."

Her father breathed deeply, sat forward, and drilled at his desk blotter with his pen.

"Carole, in the first place you haven't known him long enough to know whether you're in love with him or not."

"Before you go on to the second place, please let me dispose of that. I *am in love* with him. You haven't heard me say that since I came of age, have you? This one isn't just for laughs. It's

122

taken me a long time to feel like this, maybe because you set an example that's hard for most fellows to compete with."

Angelworth flushed with pleasure, but shook his head.

"Well, you can still pardon me for being a little sceptical. You've known this man for almost a whole day—"

"And I've never met anybody like him before."

Angelworth suddenly gave her a penetrating, almost brutal look.

"I'm sure you haven't," he said.

She bridled.

"I'm not sure what you mean by that."

"Simon Templar is not exactly unknown to me. By reputation. In fact he's . . . I can't use any other word . . . notorious."

Carole stood up.

"Notorious!" she exclaimed unbelievingly. "What do you mean, notorious? And how do you know? Have you been checking up on him because he took me out?"

Angelworth raised a soothing hand.

"Dick checked on him, dear. It wasn't very difficult. The name didn't register when I first met him last night, but it came back to me later. I don't want to upset you, but the man's . . . well, an adventurer. I can almost guarantee that his 'business' tonight wouldn't be approved by the Chamber of Commerce. And the longer he stays here, the more likely he is to get in serious trouble."

Hyram Angelworth was not prepared for his daughter's reaction. Her lips began to quiver, and her eyes brimmed with tears. And if there was one thing that everybody knew about Hyram Angelworth, it was that he could not bear to see his daughter unhappy. He was not one of those rich men who doles out handsome allowances to his offspring as a substitute for love. His actions and attitudes had made it clear ever since his wife had died that his lavish generosity to his daughter was an expression of a love that focussed exclusively on her. He had no other children.

Now he had no wife, and any women in his life were hired conveniences rather than objects of affection.

So when he saw his daughter about to cry, Angelworth got spontaneously to his feet and hurried to put his arms round her.

"Are you telling me he's a crook or something?" Carole asked, holding stiffly back from co-operating in the embrace, and struggling to control her voice.

"He pretends to be some sort of modern Robin Hood." Angelworth looked into Carole's face as he let his arm slip away from her shoulder. "Simon Templar is well known to operate on both sides of the law, taking the law into his own hands. He may have some misguided good intentions, but that doesn't alter the fact that he thinks nothing of breaking the law. Somehow or other he seems to have gotten away with it very well, financially; but that's no excuse for him either."

"Well, at least he has *some* excuse! What about Richard?" Carole pointed in the general direction of the absent Hamlin. "He's a convicted criminal, but you trust him."

"That's different," her father said. "I investigated him, got to know him, proved him over a long period, decided to give him a chance, promoted him gradually. And I'm not married to him, which is apparently what you have in mind with Simon Templar."

"You might as well be married to Richard," Carole retorted. "He's round here day and night."

Angelworth shook his head and paced across the room and back.

"It disappoints me very much to see us on the verge of quarrelling with one another," he said in a new, deeper, quieter voice. "I'm only thinking of what's best for you, but I can understand that it's hard for you to see the other side of the picture—"

"But if what you've told me is true, the police would have done something about it."

"They've been trying to, for years. I suppose you didn't con-

124

nect his real name with things you must have read in the papers. They usually call him 'The Saint.'"

It was almost as if he had struck her physically with the revelation.

"Oh, no!" she breathed. "The Saint . . ."

"Dick Hamlin thinks—and I agree—that if he has any business here, it's liable to have something to do with our local crime boss, the 'Supremo.' And you wouldn't want to get involved with that, on any side."

Her eyes were wide, but the rest of her face was still blank with shock, a mask behind which her father tried vainly to read her innermost feelings.

"Carole, there are dozens of men in this town who'd give their right arms for a second glance from you—men with good solid backgrounds, homes, big futures ahead of them."

"You know how they've always bored me," she said, as if she was barely listening.

Angelworth stood up and raised both arms in a gesture of exasperation. "I can't believe what I'm hearing. You've known this man for approximately one day, and I've just explained to you that he's a dubious character. Why don't you at least take the attitude I took with Dick Hamlin? Before you go overboard, find out what he's like. For a start, does he feel the same way about you that you feel about him?"

"Yes, I think so," Carole answered, with a kind of toneless impatience.

"Has he told you?"

"Not exactly, but I can tell."

He scrutinised her then with an intensity that made her drop her gaze to the floor. "Have you aready . . . become seriously involved with him?"

The connotation of the question was not lost on her.

"Yes," she lied. "I'll admit I threw myself at him. And I'll die if I don't see him again."

Angelworth sighed and went back to his desk chair.

125

"Good heavens, the man's just a little late getting home to-night. You can bet it isn't the first time in his life, and it won't be the last!"

"I know something's happened to him," she said flatly. "I just know it. He's in trouble . . . and now that you've said what you've said about him, I'm more worried about him than ever."

Without any warning, tears suddenly overflowed. She sank into the chair Richard Hamlin had vacated, let her arms and head rest on her father's desk, and began to sob.

Hyram Angelworth had never seen her cry since her mother had died, and he was dismayed. Like many men who have risen to the top of the power game, he was unnerved by feminine emotion. And his devotion to Carole was the most utterly genuine and unselfish thing in his life.

"What can I do, Carole?" His own voice was unsteady. "What can I possibly do?"

"You can help me, Daddy." She raised her head a little and looked at him with reddened, flooded eyes. "If I call the police they'll just laugh at me. But you know everybody. They respect you. You've given I don't know how much to police charities, and your committee . . . how could they turn you down on any-thing? Find out if they know anything about Simon trying to take on the Supremo. Or work with him."

Her father did not want to risk bringing on another cloud-burst with more discussion.

"All right," he said. "I'll do what I can, but I'm afraid most personal friends of mine will be in bed by now."

Carole stood up, dabbing her eyes.

"Thank you, Daddy." She kissed him on the cheek. "Just come tell me as soon as you hear anything, no matter what time it is."

"Well, I hope we're not going to have to sit up all night be-cause of this," Angelworth said, with a composure he did not feel.

As he watched her go, he was trying to adjust himself to the discovery that underneath the bright brittle front she presented to the world she had a secret half that he had never known or understood.

Carole passed through the living-room with hardly a glance at Richard Hamlin, who sat there turning the pages of a glossy magazine, and gave him a purely perfunctory "Good night." But she felt certain in her own mind that a few seconds before he must have been listening at the study door.

CHAPTER 7

The Saint's exiled consciousness made a slow and hobbling return. First he became vaguely aware that he was waking up, although at first he saw and heard nothing, and when he opened his eyes he was surprised, for just an instant, to see dusty, scuffed wood instead of the sheets of his bed. Then he felt the pain caused by some diabolical throbbing engine trying to drill up through the roof of his skull. That, after a moment's puzzlement, brought back to his mind a sharp memory of the fight in the private office of The Pear Tree, and the blow that had knocked him out of action.

How long had he been unconscious? Now he remembered the one previous moment of awareness, when something had pricked his arm, and he realised that he must have been injected with some drug designed to keep him comatose for the convenience of his captors.

With the past gradually forming a pattern in his mind, the Saint began to take in more of his surroundings than just the dusty boards on which his cheek rested. He started to move, to pick himself up off the floor; and discovered that his wrists were tied behind him. His legs were also immobilised by ropes, as he could see when he gingerly pressed his chin towards his chest and looked down the length of his body. He felt as if his brain had come loose within his skull and had the weight of a cannon-ball; nevertheless he clenched his teeth together and endured the pain that resulted from the movements he had to make in order to see round the room.

It was not large, about the size of an ordinary living-room, but with a much higher ceiling, so that he guessed it was part of a big building, possibly an old warehouse. The walls as well as the floors were made of rough wood. Below the tin ceiling hung a single light-bulb. There were no windows. The only things in the room besides himself, other than an interested roach or two, were a few plywood packing crates. A door at the other end of the room was closed.

Simon lay back and listened. In the distance he heard the growl of a truck labouriously gearing up from a crawl to higher speeds. Then he heard a rattle at the door and quickly closed his eyes. His captors wouldn't be so likely to give him another sleeping shot if he seemed to be still out.

He could hear the door open, and the footsteps of one man stepping inside the room, pausing, then retreating. Simon waited and at the last moment raised his eyelids just enough to get a glimpse of a broad-backed giant—standard-issue size of the Supremo's army—retreating over the threshold. He closed his eyes completely again as the guard started to turn and lock the door behind him.

At almost the same moment Simon heard a new sound: the whistle of a tugboat shrilling its work-signals to another, which replied with a quick pair of toots. So he had to be somewhere down by a river or a harbour. The watery neighbourhood conjured up an unpleasant picture of Simon Templar clad in a cement suit, sinking swiftly to a muddy end in the company of old tires, slime-covered bottles, and abandoned bedsprings.

Being very fond of Simon Templar, Simon Templar wanted to do his best to save him from such an unglamourous fate. One possibility was to talk himself out of the situation. He was still, after all, the ostensible representative of that great power West Coast Kelly—unless he had since been identified as the Saint. But even that would not have automatically ruled out the possibility that he could be connected in some pragmatic way with West Coast Kelly. That is, if Kelly had not yet disclaimed any connection. Or even—such being the Machiavellian ways of gangland—if he had . . .

But what if nobody would listen? What if there *was* nobody to listen, except some pinheaded baboon blindly carrying out orders for completing the liquidation of his prisoner?

It seemed prudent not to depend entirely on diplomatic skills, but to start looking for a more direct way to get out of the mess. A man bound hand and foot does not have much bargaining power if the higher-ups have already consigned him to the disposal unit.

Simon, hoping that his luck would prevent the guard from coming back too soon, began to search for some way of freeing himself. His mind always worked fast, leaping fences on the mount of intuition while logical processes trotted obediently along in the rear. It was the packing cases that would save him. He began to roll and squirm across the floor towards the nearest of them, and already he could see the points of the nails which he had known must have been left protruding when the crates were pried open. Getting his wrists up against one of the nails, he could painstakingly pick away at the ropes, fibre by fibre, until he was free.

Then he saw that fortune had been even kinder than he had imagined: The nearest crate had been reinforced on the outside by binding it with straps of thin flexible metal, whose edges, along the open side of the box, where they had been cut through, stood clear of the wood. The strip of steel, or whatever it was, would not be as sharp as a knife blade by any means, but it could, given enough time, serve the same purpose.

The Saint's sense of balance had not been helped by the thump he had taken on his head or the drug that had been administered to keep him asleep, but he managed to get himself into a sitting position with his back to the packing case. Then his fingers, numb for lack of circulation, sought the metal strip. The edge was disappointingly dull. He anxiously fumbled for some ragged spot which would speed up the work but found none. All he could do was move the binding of rope patiently up and down against the metal, rocking his body forward and back to increase the motion.

He could hear rather than feel his progress. After about five minutes his wrists were still as immobilised as ever, but his ears could detect the occasional snapping of a taut strand of rope fibre as it gave way to the friction of the metal. Another five minutes, same situation. How much progress had he made? He had no way of telling.

Then there were footsteps outside the door. He hurled himself away from the crate, rolled over so that his back and arms and the partially severed rope could not be seen from the entrance to the room. There was no time to get back to the spot where his captors had originally left him, which meant that he could not pretend to be still unconscious. Momentarily he experienced a sinking feeling of despair. He had come so close.

But the door did not open. The sound of shoes on wood moved away. Now there had to be another inchworm trip to the crate. Once more Simon got himself into a sitting position and resumed the scraping of his bonds against the strip of metal. Now he worked faster, his body pumping forward and back like an engine under a full head of steam. Sweat ran from his forehead into his eyes. Dust tickled his nose and forced him to struggle continually not to sneeze—a sound that might bring the guard hurrying to look in on him.

At last he felt a loosening of the pressure on his wrists. Ferociously he dragged the last strands of rope up and down against the metal until he felt them break completely.

His arms were free. Shaking the rope away, he worked his fingers to restore the warmth and feeling and strength to them. On his wrists were the white, bloodless indentations the bonds had made. In another minute he had untied the rope that had held his ankles together. It was like coming from a black and airless cave out into the light.

But he still had a long way to go. He tossed the wrist rope behind the packing case and got to his feet, testing his unsteady legs as he went back to the place where he had been lying when he regained consciousness. Should he lie down, loosely wrap the rope back round his ankles, and try to take the guard or guards by surprise when they came for him? Or should he wait by the door and launch an attack the instant it opened?

It would have taken him only a few seconds to make the decision; but in even less time than that, without any warning, the door abruptly opened and the huge guard walked into the room.

A direct quotation of what the guard said when he saw Simon Templar untied in the middle of the room is fortunately not essential to the substance of this history. Simon did not bother to reply. All his attention and energy were concentrated on getting to the guard before the guard's beefy hand could get to the gun that hung in harness over his heart.

The Saint did manage that, but he had not reckoned with the stiffness of his legs after their long confinement, and his movements were comparatively slow and clumsy. The fist he threw at the guard's Neanderthal jaw was parried by a tree-trunk arm, while the man's other hand slammed out awkwardly at the Saint's chest. If the gorilla had not himself been taken aback with startlement, it might have shaped into a counter-punch that could have put Simon out again, but instead of launching a counter-attack against him, Simon's prognathous opponent was only trying to fend him off, shouting: "Hey, hold on! I come to let you loose!"

"You're *what?*" Simon whooped.

"Yeah! I just come to let you loose!"

The big lug was making no effort to go for his gun. Backing off a little, with both hands out in front of him, he could have passed for a professional wrestling villain going through the melodramatics of pleading for mercy.

131

Simon relaxed just a little.

"You mean I can leave?" he asked.

"Yeah. That's right. Yeah."

"Under my own power? I can go where I want?"

The guard nodded. "You can go."

They stood facing one another in silence.

"Well," the guard said, "go on and go."

"Would you mind going ahead of me?"

The guard backed out the door, and Simon followed him into —as he had suspected—the main area of a warehouse. It, like the smaller room, held nothing more interesting than empty crates.

"How did you get untied?" the guard asked.

"Tied?" Simon asked, wickedly. "I never was tied."

A frown began at the guard's crew-cut hairline and spread down over the rest of his wide face. "Whatta you mean you wasn't tied? Sure you was tied."

"No, I wasn't."

The guard pointed at him and said desperately: "Now look, you was tied, and don't tell me you wasn't tied."

"Okay," Simon said with a smile. "I was just kidding. But I sure am grateful to whoever it was that untied me."

The goon had started to relax, but now his face crinkled again, like the face of an extremely large baby about to erupt into squalls.

"You're tellin' me some*body* untied you? Who do ya think—"

"I don't know who he was," Simon said nonchalantly. "Little guy." He indicated with one palm very near the floor. "About so high. Two or three feet. Green pointed hat and a long white beard. Do you know him?"

"You're pullin' my leg," the guard announced warily, after a moment's consideration. "Nobody could have gotten in there anyways because I was right out here the whole time."

"Whatever you say," Simon murmured. "Now, I'd appreciate it if you'd tell me why you're letting me go."

"They just come and tole me to let you go. They didn't give no reason or nothin' else."

"Who come?" Simon queried, feeling like part of the cast of a Tarzan movie.

"Never mind who come," the guard said belligerently. "Never mind anything. Just beat it!"

"I just wondered why anybody would go to all the trouble to give me a room for the night and then kick me out of it before morning. It is before morning, isn't it? Somebody seems to have mislaid my wristwatch."

"Probably that little green guy," the guard said, and grinned with glee at his own wit. He looked at his wrist. "It's one o'clock in the middle of the night. Now would you beat it so I can get home and get some sleep?"

"I don't suppose I could have my gun back?" Simon asked.

"I ain't got your gun or nothin' else."

Simon went to the door.

"Could you tell me where I am?" he enquired. "It might help me to get somewhere else."

"You're on the River, and you're lucky you ain't in it, so get goin'."

"Well, thanks for the hospitality. Your floor's very comfortable but your roaches need polishing."

He glanced back and saw the guard picking up the discarded length of rope, from which he would try to unravel the mystery of the Saint's escape.

CHAPTER 8

If the guard had something to be briefly puzzled about, the Saint had much more. As he walked out of the dark neighbourhood of warehouses and loading ramps—noting that the place where he had been held was marked CONDEMNED—PHILADELPHIA FIRE DEPARTMENT—his mind kept sifting the information he had so far, and getting nowhere. It didn't make any sense at all that the group at The Pear Tree, who knew him as a man who had attacked a couple of their members the night before and burst into their communications centre demanding to see their Most High and Secret Leader, knew him as a potential if not a present danger, and had him in their clutches, would have tossed him casually back into the stream like a minnow not worth bothering about.

It was enough to wound a lesser man's pride, but the Saint was already thinking of his next move. And that would be to backtrack and take up where he had left off a few hours before. Presumably he might be in an even better position now to negotiate as the representative of West Coast Kelly, or at least no worse. When he finally found a cab, he directed it straight back to The Pear Tree.

But even from the window of the taxi he could see that the place was dark.

"Do they usually shut down by one o'clock?" Simon asked the driver.

"Naw. More like four o'clock. Ain't that a sign on the door?"

Simon got out, crossed the sidewalk, and looked at the card taped under the brass name plate.

THE MANAGEMENT REGRETS THAT THE PEAR TREE WILL BE CLOSED TEMPORARILY FOR REDECORATING.

He knocked on the door anyway, just in case somebody should still be round, but there was no response. When he got back to the New Sylvania, he phoned The Pear Tree's number; there was no answer.

He walked to one of the windows of his room, looked out over the lights of the city, and pondered the enigma: closed for redecorating. Just like a prodded turtle drawing in its head and legs. And all because of one man? Had he been recognised as the Saint? Even if he had, it didn't add up. Simon felt that somewhere he must have missed a pointer, a hint that would put some meaning into apparently senseless events. He felt that an embryonic answer was stirring somewhere in his subconscious, but he could not dredge it to the surface. He was too tired, still a little dopey from the drug. Tomorrow it would all be clearer.

He was checking the night latch on his door when his phone rang. Maybe this would be it, his mysterious opponent's next move.

"Simon!" Carole cried. "Where have you been? I've been worried sick. Are you all right? Didn't you get my messages?"

"About five minutes ago, when I came in," Simon said. "But I thought it was too late to call you. Why aren't you asleep?"

"Asleep?" Carole said incredulously. "How on earth could I sleep? What happened to you?"

Simon chose his words carefully.

"I was detained. Unavoidably detained. Circumstances beyond my control. I'm just sorry you got upset."

"Upset isn't the word for it. I even had Daddy calling the police about you. Did they find you?"

"No. I found myself. Wasn't that a little alarmist? What did you think had happened to me? You're the potential kidnap victim, remember. Nobody would pay any ransom for me."

"I didn't know what had happened, but I was going crazy. What was it 'detained' you?"

"I'll tell you all about it tomorrow. Now you can call off the constabulary and we can all get some sleep."

Her voice dropped with disappointment.

"Can't you come up and tell me now?"

"I don't think your papa would approve. Not at this hour of the morning. And I'm not feeling too bright right now. Some of these business conferences leave you with a thick head."

"You're mad at me," she sulked.

"No. I'll meet you for lunch tomorrow. How about that?"

She had to agree. They made the arrangements, but she was reluctant to hang up.

Her lingering gave Simon a chance to ask a question that was suddenly hammering for release.

"Your father really called the police?"

"Yes; I begged him to do it. He has a lot of friends there. He's done a lot for them."

"Who was it he called?"

"I don't know," Carole said. "I wasn't in the room. Does it matter?"

"No," he answered softly. "It doesn't matter. Good night now."

"Good night," she said. "I love you."

Simon settled the telephone slowly into its cradle and sat for a long time without moving. In his stomach there was a sinking, almost sick feeling.

Nobody knew that he had been missing last night, except the back-room boys at The Pear Tree . . . and Carole Angelworth. Therefore, nobody outside the Angelworth household could have ordered, or induced the Supremo to order his release. Therefore the Supremo had to be actually in the Police Department, or . . .

Angelworth. Even the name was too good to be true, just like its charitable possessor. Simon had tended to assume until now that the Supremo was a secluded figure, personally remote from publicity, working through front men. But the Supremo could just as well be a man known in public life, a man whose popular image was in sharp contrast to the secret sources of his power . . . a man like Hyram Angelworth.

Man . . . Of course he was consciously, even forcibly, confining his speculations to the conventional gender. Beautiful young girls didn't lead secret double lives as the rulers of criminal empires, except in the most extravagant kinds of fiction.

A likelier possibility flickered across the screen of the Saint's imagination: Richard Hamlin, as Angelworth's confidential secretary or whatever he was, would be in a unique position to exploit and manipulate Angelworth's financial power and political influence. This might be a case of a power behind the throne . . . unknown even to the occupant of the throne? And Hamlin already had a criminal record. A lot of writers would go for that.

And just as many would trail him round as a red herring.

Certainly Hamlin wouldn't be blinded by any romantic infatuation like Carole's. Could he have some complicated idea of
trading on that infatuation to ingratiate himself? That would also
be one for the books; but people sometimes had strange weak-
nesses.

All right—what purely practical motive could the Supremo
have had for letting the Saint go?

The only explanation that Simon could come up with along
that line was that the Supremo, overruling The Pear Tree
quorum, had decided that West Coast Kelly's supposed proposi-
tion should at least be given a hearing, and without the prejudi-
cial factor of a maltreated ambassador. Which meant that West
Coast Kelly had not yet disowned the Saint—or that the accredi-
tation would take longer to obtain. Meanwhile the situation
would be left in the suspended animation of "don't-call-us-we'll-
call-you."

With a corollary that the Saint, unlike the Supremo, could
only be the loser in that kind of waiting game.

But even the fascination of those mental jigsaw puzzles could
not keep him from sleep much longer.

CHAPTER 9

When Simon Templar got out of bed a little later that morning,
he had added one more theory to his entanglement of teasers. It
was almost as bizarre as the others, and yet he found it the hard-
est to eliminate.

What his conscious mind had not been able to accept the
night before, his subconscious had relentlessly and imperson-
ally crystallised while he slept. His surface thinking had been
blurred and distorted by what he wished to be true. It had trod-
den gingerly, picking its way like a mountain climber crossing a
snowfield. But in the relaxed transition back to wakefulness he

137

had felt the white glaze give way beneath his feet, and he had plunged into the crevasse.

It was a little before ten o'clock when he walked into Lieutenant Stacey's office, after reaching one of the toughest decisions he had ever had to make, and his expression darkly reflected his feelings. He could easily have put a cheerful mask on his face, but candour served his purposes at this point.

Stacey reacted to the Saint's appearance with something as close to alarm as his cool, almost scholarly face could manage. The freckles stood out more vividly in contrast to his pale skin. Some people have a problem with blushing; Lieutenant Stacey was embarrassed by the fact that he turned extremely white under pressure.

"What's wrong?" he asked.

"What's wrong?" Simon said emotionally, and sat down. "I'll tell you what's wrong. I almost got killed last night."

Without waiting for any more questions, he told the story of his visit to The Pear Tree, his captivity, and his release.

Stacey blinked.

"I'd say you were very lucky," he managed. "I was afraid something like that would happen. What could one man do against a bunch like that? The only thing that beats me is that they let you go."

"It wasn't exactly what I'd expected either," the Saint rejoined. "How do you explain it?"

Stacey held a freshly sharpened yellow pencil upright between his thumb and forefinger and stared at it.

"I don't," he admitted after a moment, and let the pencil fall over on to his desk top. "That organisation can swallow men up like quicksand. One foot in, and that's the last you hear of them. How do *you* explain the special treatment?"

"My innocent boyish charm?" Simon suggested. "Or maybe they'd run out of bullets and couldn't find a knife at that hour of the night. Whatever it is, I'm not giving them a second chance. I'm out."

He stood up abruptly. Stacey, in surprise, automatically rose from his own chair.

"I don't get you," he said. "What are you doing next?"

"Minding my own business," said the Saint. "And staying alive if possible. If anybody asks about me, say I'm in Tahiti."

"Is that what you want me to tell Brad Ryner?" Stacey asked. There was the faintest trace of accusation in his tone.

"You can tell Brad the truth," Simon said. "Tell him I just can't go on, now that I've got a good idea what I'm up against."

And like a failure in battle who did not want to face his comrades, the Saint turned round and stalked out of the office.

He went straight back to the New Sylvania and began to pack. With that done, he would be able to leave immediately after lunch, and the last thing he wanted was to hang round under that roof. But having nothing else to hurry for before noon, his suitcase was still half empty on the bed when his telephone rang.

"This is Brad Ryner," the voice on the line said. "Stacey told me what happened. I've gotta see you."

"Is it really necessary? Didn't you hear? I chickened out."

The detective summed up in one elegant syllable what he thought of that.

"Yeah, it's necessary," he went on. "You can at least talk to me for five minutes can't you?"

"If you say so. I'll come over to the hospital—"

"I'll come to your place," Ryner interrupted. "I'm not at the hospital. I just snuck out the back way and I'm in a phone booth. I'll be over there in a couple minutes."

He did not give Simon a chance to protest. He had also conveniently underestimated the time it would take him to get to the hotel, no doubt to be sure Simon had no excuse for leaving. It was twenty minutes later when he knocked at the door.

When Simon turned the knob he was confronted by a mummy in a raincoat. Most of Brad Ryner's face was still swathed in bandages. In one hand he carried a briefcase and with the other hand he supported himself against the doorjamb. Simon helped him into the room.

"Watch my ribs," Ryner groaned. "I've got more fractures than San Francisco after the earthquake."

"And you crawled out of that hosptial bed and dragged yourself over here? You must have more cracks in your skull than you do in your ribs."

"Never mind about me," Ryner said as soon as he had been carefully deposited on one of the sofas. "What about you? What's all this stuff about you being scared? You've never been scared in your life!"

"Everybody gets smart sometime," Simon said grimly. "I'm sorry. That's all I can say."

"You can say more than that," Ryner growled with painful effort. "You are not scared. I know that! You are not scared, and so there's some other reason why you're backing out. What is it?"

"The fortunetelling machine's downstairs on the sidewalk," Simon said. "I don't answer questions when you put a penny in."

"Then I'll put a boot in, right where it hurts," Ryner retorted angrily.

"For a man who can hardly stand up you're talking mighty big," Simon said with rigid control.

"Yeah, well I don't mean that. I mean this." Ryner beat his fingers against his closely held briefcase. "I think you found out something last night that made you back off. You wouldn't go over to the other side. If somebody threatened you, it'd just make you madder. I know you're after a fast buck, but you wouldn't let nobody buy you off. So what is it? The way I figure it, it's gotta be one of two things: You're a businessman. Maybe you found out you could make a bigger killing if you took another route. And the other thing is, which I believe is the truth, the other thing is that you're covering for somebody. Maybe somebody they can get at that you can't protect. Or maybe you found out some friend of yours is mixed up with 'em."

"You're very clever," Simon said. "You should be a detective."

"Not funny," Ryner rasped. "If you got soft on that gang for some reason, it's gotta be because you don't realise what's really going on. Open up this briefcase, wouldja, and look at what's inside. My hands ain't working too good on zippers; they never do after somebody's walked on my knuckles."

Simon took the plastic case from the other man, who sank back exhausted against the sofa cushions.

"What am I going to look at?"

"Get ready to get sick," Ryner said. "You're gonna see just how the great Supremo operates."

From the briefcase Simon took a thick set of eight-by-ten photographs, and what he saw as he went through them made even a man as hardened to violence as the Saint feel sickness gnawing and clawing at his insides.

"Not just a slug in some punk's gut, huh?" Ryner said. "Not just a cop with a couple broken ribs. Look at it! Acid and knives. That's what they like best. Especially the acid."

Simon turned one of the photographs towards him.

"This girl," he said. "She couldn't be more than ten years old."

"Nine," Ryner affirmed. "She's the daughter of a judge who wouldn't play ball. She'll never see out of that eye. I think the other young girl there was luckier. She didn't make it. A girl's not going to have much of a life if men can't stand to look at her face."

The butchery and mutilation shown in the police photographs had more of an effect on Simon than hours of argument could have done. He had been thinking, until now, in terms of inter-racket shakedowns, vice monopolies, crooked political manoeuvres, and real-estate hanky-panky. Now he was brought face to face, on the most brutal personal level, with the products of power combined with uninhibited ferocity.

"Do you want to hear about some of the other cute tricks they've pulled?" Ryner asked.

"No," Simon said.

He put the pictures back into the briefcase. If the Supremo could have seen the Saint's face or heard the sound of his voice there would have been considerable unease in the City of Brotherly Love at that moment.

"Are you still gonna back out?" Ryner insisted.

"No."

"Well, so what are you gonna do?"

"Don't push me," said the Saint. "I never thought I'd have to make the toughest choice of my life twice in one day. Just let me know where I can contact you later, this afternoon. I've got a date to keep first."

Simon no longer wanted to meet Carole for lunch but he knew that he had to. She threw her arms round him happily when she got out of her taxi at the William Penn Grill, where he was waiting for her, forcing the noontime river of surging protoplasm to wash round them on the sidewalk. The air was fresh and crisp after the recent rains. Brilliant sunshine brought dazzling highlights to Carole's long blond hair, which was obviously fresh from the attentions of a beauty parlor. A heavy drizzling overcast and impenetrable fog would have been more suitable to the Saint's mood, but now he put on the false face he had not worn in Lieutenant Stacey's office. He had plenty of deception ahead of him, so he might just as well start now.

"Last night I wondered if I'd ever see you again," Carole was chattering happily, squeezing his hand as they went in. "I really did. Now here we are. And I'm simply dying to hear your story about last night. It had better be good!"

It was impossible to put her off for longer than it took to order cocktails.

"I'm afraid it's terribly dull," he said. "But it makes me feel pretty stupid. I had to look up these . . . business connections, and I found they had rather riotous ideas about conferences. They had to show me the town as a warm-up. And I ended up losing track of the time. To put it bluntly, I was out cold for a while."

"I would have thought," she said meditatively, "that the Saint had a stronger head than that."

He was able to keep his mask expressionless.

"What saint?"

"It's no good," she said, and her eyes were still twinkling. "I know who you are. You were mean not to tell me yourself."

"Who did tell you?"

"My father. He thought he recognised the name, and he checked it up. Or Dick Hamlin did. They always worry about me."

"But it didn't worry you?"

"I was thrilled. So long as you weren't getting murdered somewhere . . . Now, what *did* really happen last night?"

"Just what I've told you, skipping the gory details. On my honour," he told her truthfully.

Her eyes would not shift from his face.

"Well, do you have to have any more of these conferences?"

He rubbed his brow ruefully.

"I should hope not. I'd rather retire in one piece, if I thought I could afford to."

"You could afford to." Her fingers lay on his wrist, only for a moment. "I see I'll have to show you how to enjoy life."

Somehow he got through the lunch. Carole's thoughts were all on the future—tomorrow, next week, next month. She pictured herself and Simon together at the theatre, on rides, at parties, on country walks, sprawled in front of a fireplace in the evening. Simon's thoughts were walled in by this single day, whose ending would form a stone barrier between him and Carole. He knew how she would really feel tomorrow, and it would not be as she now imagined.

But he smiled and laughed and asked questions, while evading answering any himself. He did caution her that his life wasn't a long vacation . . . that he was going to have things to do and places to go in the weeks to come. Nothing so minor as that could squelch her exuberance. Life was just beginning. Give her a chance, and she could make anything possible.

When Carole fell she fell hard, and there was nothing the Saint could do now to cushion the crash at the bottom.

He wanted to end his own ordeal as quickly as possible. Her bright blue eyes, her soft expressive lips, were working at his defences like the summer sun on a block of ice. He could not look at her without a shattering impulse to take her in his arms and kiss her.

"I'm afraid I'll have to cut this short," he told her over coffee. "If I'm going to take a holiday, I've got some loose ends I must tidy up first."

"You said you'd had enough of those conferences."

"Of last night's kind, yes. This one is a bit different."

She took a gold cigarette-case from her purse, and a cigarette from it.

"Is it getting rid of that other woman?" she accused, less seriously.

"Not only her, but all the children," he said glibly, and gave her a light from the match booklet on the table. "By the way, does your father know you're out with me now?"

"Yes, of course."

"And he didn't object?"

"Yes, of course."

"I see. But he'll be pacing up and down till you get home safely."

"They say that walking's wonderful exercise for men of his age—"

She broke off as another man materialised seemingly from nowhere beside their table. From being perplexed, she became dumbfounded as he sat down quietly in the vacant chair opposite her and proffered an open wallet that displayed a badge and an identity card.

"Police Department." He took the cigarette from her fingers and stubbed it out in the ashtray. "I believe this contains marijuana, and that you have others like it in your possession. You are under arrest, and will be formally charged at Headquarters."

"Are you out of your mind?" Carole exploded. "Do you know who I am?"

"You bet I do, lady. We've been watching you for quite some time. Now will you come quietly, or will I beckon up some help and we can all get our pictures in the papers?"

"This has got to be a mistake," Simon protested. "I didn't smell any marijuana when I lit that cigarette—and I know the smell. She's got a right to call a lawyer—"

The look that Lieutenant Stacey turned on him was as cold as if they had never met.

"After we've booked her, smarty. Or you can do it for her as soon as we've left. Unless you'd rather come along too, and be charged with aiding, abetting, conspiring, and anything else we might think up."

Carole turned to stare at the Saint in blank desperation.

"Don't get yourself in dutch, Simon," she said huskily. "This has got to be a frame-up. Get in touch with my father. He'll know what to do."

"Okay," the Saint promised stonily, knowing precisely what that acquiescence would mean.

CHAPTER 10

Hyram Angelworth lounged in an armchair in his living-room idly scanning *The Wall Street Journal* to the accompaniment of soft music from the record player. He did not hear a sound beyond the strains of Guy Lombardo until a firm, resonant voice almost at his elbow said, "Good evening, Hyram."

For a split second it seemed to him that the voice must have come from the radio, since he was alone in the apartment. But as his hands jerked the newspaper with surprise, and he looked up, he saw that he was not alone. Simon Templar stood next to him, tall and grim, but as relaxed as if they had just met by chance in the street.

"What are you doing in here?" Angelworth spluttered. "How did you get into my apartment?"

"Generally I walk through walls, but in this case it was simpler: I borrowed your daughter's key for a few minutes and had a duplicate made. She didn't know it of course. She's too fond of you for that, poor misguided girl."

Angelworth dropped the paper to the floor as he stood up. His voice was unsteady.

"Where is Carole? Isn't she here? She said she was going to lunch with you."

Angelworth was looking round as if someone else must surely have entered the room with Simon.

"Your daughter's social life isn't what I've come to talk to you about," said the Saint. "I'll let you have it very straight: I know this is the Supremo's address, and I'm here to talk to the Supremo."

"Supremo?" Hyram Angelworth said in a soft incredulous voice. He looked as Santa Claus might look if accused of being Beelzebub in disguise. "You mean the gangster?"

"That's right," Simon replied. "King Sin himself. I can't say I've been dying to meet him, but I nearly did. As you damn well know."

Hyram Angelworth raised both hands piously and backed away, shaking his head. Simon recognised a fellow actor. Angelworth was having trouble deciding between laughing at the absurdity of the accusation and flying into a rage because of it.

"There's just no point carrying this on any further," he protested. "You're talking to the wrong man."

Simon allowed himself a few dramatics of his own. He leaned forward and brought his fist down fiercely on the back of the chair Angelworth had just vacated.

"Now, look," he shouted. "I haven't got time to waste on those games! You're not talking to one of your bootlicking ward-heelers. Listen to what I'm telling you, Angelworth: I come from West Coast Kelly. He's twice as big as you'll ever be, and he's going to be bigger soon because he's going to merge you into his business. While you've been sitting round getting fat, he's been taking up your slack and buying up some of your boys. In other words, he's taking over your operation, and if you're willing to talk turkey and come to terms you won't do too badly. We're not greedy. We just want some co-operation."

"How can I co-operate when I don't even know what you're talking about?" Angelworth argued. "I'd suggest you get out of here before I call the police."

He went over to a table and placed his hand on the telephone there.

"I'd suggest you don't bother," Simon told him. "I know I'm in the right place—never mind how. So if you could cut the phoney theatricals we could get down to business."

Suddenly Angelworth's right hand dipped into the drawer of the table and came out holding a pistol.

The Saint made no effort to stop him or counter the move. He smiled happily.

"I'm very glad you did that," he said. "You just told me I'm right."

"I should have let the boys finish you when they had you last night," Angelworth said.

All the innocence had vanished from his face and all the honey from his voice.

"You've really let yourself in for it now," he snarled. "Breaking into my apartment with a stolen key—who could blame me for shooting in self-defence? And if that West Coast Mick has any ideas about butting into my affairs, what happens to you should be a good warning to him!"

"I'm disappointed in you, Hyram," Simon murmured. "Maybe Richard Hamlin really is the brains behind this outfit. It looks

147

like you couldn't think your way across the street in the rush hour."

Angelworth's hand tightened on the automatic.

"What's that supposed to mean?"

"You've forgotten about Carole. That's why I didn't bring her back with me."

The older man was visibly staggered. The colour drained from his face.

"Carole," he whispered. "You wouldn't hurt her . . ."

"Why not? It'd only be taking a page from your book. There was a certain judge's daughter, for example. I don't think a splash of vitriol would improve Carole's complexion any."

"Don't you know it was only because of her you were turned loose last night?"

"I guessed that. And so I wouldn't want to hurt her—so long as you play ball."

Even to an enemy the expression on Angelworth's face was harrowing. He suddenly looked years older. The hand that held the automatic was slowly lowered until his arm hung limply at his side.

Then a new voice was heard: "It's okay, Mr. Angelworth. I've got him covered."

They both turned to see Richard Hamlin, with a pistol of his own, coming into the living-room from another door. Hamlin looked very pleased with himself. He was obviously more at home juggling account books than guns, but he liked the role of man of action.

"I'm afraid it won't do any good," Angelworth said heavily. "They have Carole. I've got to do whatever they want."

He turned back to Simon.

"So what is it you want . . . to set her free, without hurting her?"

"I told you," Simon said. "Your co-operation. You can start by proving your good faith—handing over your records, giving us a run-down on all your, ah, enterprises. Then West Coast

Kelly will tell you how much he wants. There must be some very special files. A hidden safe, maybe?"

"You can't show him anything!" Hamlin said furiously. "If you do, Kelly could put us out and take everything!"

Hyram Angelworth turned desperately to Simon.

"Listen—you owe me your life. Give me mine in return, and leave Carole out of this!"

"I'm sorry," said the Saint. "I've got my orders. And Carole won't be hurt unless you force us to."

Angelworth's shoulders sagged as he let out a long deep breath.

"You leave me no choice." He turned wearily. "Come into my study."

"Wait a minute!" Hamlin barked, waving his gun. "There's more people involved than just Carole. I can't let you do it!"

"Can't *let* me do it?" Angelworth said in a dangerously quiet voice. "I decide what's done here. I pulled you out of jail and turned you from a convict into a rich man—"

"And he'll turn you back into a convict if you don't behave yourself," Simon put in. "With your record you'll make a perfect fall guy if the cops ever start suspecting your boss."

"I have decided," Angelworth said to Hamlin, "to combine forces with West Coast Kelly. Now get out of the way and let me settle this business."

Hamlin hesitated a moment, but placed himself between Angelworth and the study.

"I won't tolerate insubordination," Angelworth snapped. "Get out of the way."

"No!" Hamlin half screamed.

Angelworth shot first and sent Hamlin careening back against the wall, his gun flying from his hand and tumbling across the carpet. As Hamlin sagged to the floor, blood soaking the left side of his body, Simon had time to wonder if the secretary really would have pulled the trigger of his own pistol. He had certainly

149

been destroyed by the hesitant mentality of an employee, while Angelworth had been quickened by the mentality of the leader.

"Nice shot," said the Saint. "I see how you got to be the Supremo."

He followed Angelworth past Hamlin, who was unconscious but still bleeding, into the book-lined study. In a moment Angelworth had swung one of the bookshelves away from the wall and was opening the door of a safe which had been hidden behind it.

"All the important records are here," Angelworth said. "Take what you want and look at it."

The Saint felt triumphant relief. He took the folders which Angelworth handed him and strolled out into the living-room looking through the papers. Angelworth's eyes followed him anxiously.

Simon leaned against the wall near a window. Without taking his eyes from his reading, he pulled the curtain aside, waved his arm up and down three times, and let the curtain fall into place again. Angelworth's body stiffened.

"What was that?"

"Signaling," Simon said.

"Signaling what?"

"That everything's okay." His signal would have been received by a watcher on the roof of the building opposite, and relayed back to the floor below the New Sylvania's penthouse. He looked up from the folders. "This is interesting stuff. You're very creative with numbers. For Carole's sake I wish you'd been a math professor instead of a crook."

The door from the hallway burst open, and suddenly the room was invaded by three blue uniforms led by a man in a plain suit. Confronted with this police presence, Hyram Angelworth's instincts told him to bolt for the rear exit, but intelligence told him to try a last desperate sound.

"Thank God you've come!" he cried, pointing a shaking finger at the Saint. "This man broke in here and—"

"Spare us," said the Saint. "The law, for once, is with me." He spoke to Lieutenant Stacey, who was leading the task force. "This fine-looking gent is the Supremo. He was obliging enough to hand over the evidence from the wall safe, and to plug his assistant there for trying to stop him. Brother Hamlin seems to be alive; he should make a very willing witness."

"You're working for the police?" Angelworth grated. "Then where's Carole? What have you done with Carole?"

"She's downtown, at Police Headquarters, protected by a charming detective lieutenant. She was picked up on a phoney charge to make certain she wouldn't be in touch with you after lunch."

"Did she know?" Angelworth asked almost piteously.

"No, she didn't," Simon answered.

With incredible swiftness Angelworth spun round and dashed back into the study. As the policemen raced after him, Simon shouted: "Watch out—he's got a gun in there!"

But there was no sound of shots. A moment later, after scuffling noises, the police emerged into the living-room again with a handcuffed and crestfallen ex-Supremo in their charge.

"He was trying to kill himself," one of them said. "We got the gun just when he was putting it to his head."

"I'll give him one thing," Simon said thoughtfully. "He did love one person in the world more than himself."

The atmosphere at the airport the next noon was clear, kerosene-perfumed, and—to the Saint—supercharged with his own eagerness to get away from Philadelphia. Brad Ryner sat in the police car with the door open, and Lieutenant Stacey stood beside the Saint as a porter carried Simon's bag into the terminal.

"I want you to know how much we appreciate what you did," Stacey said earnestly.

Simon shook his head, nodding, and turned to Ryner.

"Look," Ryner said, "I feel mighty bad about this. When I

151

used those pictures to get you to help out, I didn't realise what it was gonna cost you. I mean about the girl. I didn't know what a crummy mess it would put you in, not until she told you off at headquarters last night."

The Saint's mind was forced to leap back and relive that scene again. Carole had been released, with explanations, when her father was brought in, and had then had to cope alone with the shock of his arrest and the revelations that went with it, while Simon was indulging the authorities in their mania for paperwork. It had not been necessary for him to see her even after she had helped with summoning lawyers and fending off vulturine reporters. In fact, Stacey, who was well aware of her feelings by that time, had tried to avert the unpleasantries.

Sitting in his office that evening, he had said to Simon, while Brad Ryner listened: "She's very upset, naturally. She's not being rational. She's got to blame somebody, and it's easier for her to blame you than her father. I'd suggest that you don't see her. At least not for some time, till she's cooled down."

"Yeah," Ryner had joined in. "Just blow. What good can it do to let her chew you out?"

"If she wants to see me, I at least owe her that," Simon had said. "Let her in."

It had been worse than he had anticipated. When Carole entered Stacey's office she had looked so haggard, her eyes so swollen and reddened with crying, that Simon could scarcely recognise her as the lively happy girl he had known so briefly. It was understandable. Before this she had not been able to imagine to herself that there was even a one per cent clay content in her paternal idol's feet, and now he turned out to be ninety-nine per cent pure mud. And the man she had loved was the one who had shattered her world, doomed her father to prison, and condemned her at the very least to humiliation and a terrible time of readjustment.

"You pig!" she said, and for as long as he lived he would remember the corrosive bitterness of every syllable. "I can't think of anything low enough to call you."

"Now wait a minute," Ryner had put in. "Don't blame Simon for what your father did. He was only . . ."

Simon silenced the detective with a glance, but did not try to reply to Carole himself.

"You could have told me," she said. "You knew I . . . I loved you. And all the time you were using me to get at my father!"

That was all she could say. A racking sob choked her so that no more words could get through. Simon had taken one step towards her, and then she had turned and run from the office.

Now, at the airport, Ryner was saying: "But since you did face her like that, why didn't you at least explain why you had to do it? You didn't have to let her think you're a heel. You weren't using her, the way she said."

"No, I wasn't," Simon said. "But do you think she'd believe me? It would only have sounded as if I were trying to make her father look even worse. When you've just wrecked a girl's life, all the logic in the world won't convince her that you *had* to do it. And in the long run, it'll be much better for her to go on hating me."

With a final good-bye he strode from the police car to the door of the terminal.

"Well," Stacey said, "maybe only a saint could have played it that way . . ."

And they watched him walk away into the lobby.